FREDDY'S NEW LIFE

A. Diel

This book is for all the kids who need it, who might have a feeling they don't understand and no words to describe it, and for their friends and parents to understand them a little better.

The (not quite) first day of school

❖ ❖ ❖

It was the Friday before the first day of school, and the administration had all the new students come down for an orientation. I had just moved into town and hadn't had a chance to establish any friendships yet, so I was comforted to know that all of the other students I'd meet that day would be in the same position as me. I suppose the idea was to give us an opportunity to familiarize ourselves with our new school and potentially forge alliances before being thrown into the hustle and bustle of opening day.

Feeling quite nervous, I got dropped off by my mom at the front gate of the school 15 minutes before they were expecting us "if you're 10 minutes early, you're 5 minutes late" I could almost hear my dad in my head, some of his favourite sayings still echoed so clearly.

I walked down the halls, taking in my new

surroundings, the smell of cleaning products was at the forefront of my senses, pre-semester disinfecting I assumed, by this time next week, these halls would smell of hormones and teen-age anxiety.

With every step, my shoes made that familiar squeaking sound that every student at every school knows all to well, as I continued my exploration of my new school, I examined the anti-drug, anti-bullying and pro-abstinence PSA posters that lined the walls.

As the meeting time approached, I made my way towards the administration office so that I could be introduced to the other newbies and receive my class schedule for the upcoming semester, and when I approached, I spotted a small gathering of kids my age that looked somewhat awkward, despite standing in a circle formation that is usually reserved for friends.

Hesitant, I slowed my pace, wanting to get a better feel for the vibe before walking into the proverbial firing line, just in case they were a pre-established group, looking for even "fresher" meat to make fun of, effectively making themselves less vulnerable come Monday.

There were three of them, a girl and two boys, none of them had any physical similarities, so it eliminated the possibility of siblings, and as I got closer, I could see that the taller of the boys was talking in long run-on sentences and that the other two were having a hard time getting a word in edge-wise, the forced politeness was obvious, which I assumed meant that they had all just met moments ago, recently enough for me to inject myself without being the "newcomer".

I locked eyes with the taller boy, noticing he had large brown eyes and he seemed friendly. His short blond hair was spiked at the front, which only helped him look taller. The striped blue and red polo shirt he was wearing was relatively slim fitting and I could tell that he was skinny, but definitely not scrawny. His physique was mildly imposing, but his giant smile softened him a bit, and he sensed that I was waiting for an invitation, so he waved me over and made me feel immediately welcome.

Hey dude, you new here too? Not waiting for an answer, he continued... *I'm Tristan, this is Maggie and this...* He paused, clearly searching his memory

Max... Said the other boy, sounding a little annoyed

...Right, MAX! Continued Tristan, unfazed by his blunder *What's your name?*

I hadn't expected to be put on the spot, and somehow, the three of them awaiting my response almost made me forget my own name

Umm... Frederick, but most people just call me Freddy. I managed to blurt out, while staring at my feet.

Well it's nice to meet you "umm Frederick" responded Tristan, clearly trying to be funny.

Where you from? He asked as a follow-up.

But before I could respond, a small woman with what can only be described as "bird-like" features, came out of the administration office holding a clipboard, she wore a knitted white shawl over a modest blue shirt that was loosely but neatly tucked into her ankle length skirt and she had a gold chain tied to each arm of the thin glasses that were perched on the end of her beak-like nose. She looked unpleasant and her voice matched her appearance as she opened her mouth to speak:

Right, My name is Miss Wilkins, and I am here to welcome you to your new school. She spoke in a dry, unenthusiastic tone. *The four of you will be divided into your two separate homerooms today, so that we can better show you around the school and answer all of your specific questions, so...* she paused and tilted her head back to look through her glasses at her paperwork *...Tristan Stanfield and Maggie Reynolds, you two will come with me, and...* Again, she paused to look over her clipboard... *Maximillian Longview and Frederick Miller, you will be accompanying Miss Friedman...* She paused slightly... *who appears to be running late...* the last part was mumbled sideways with a hint of derision and judgement... *so the two of you may sit quietly in the front office's waiting room until she arrives... is that understood?*

The four of us quietly nodded our heads, and with that, Miss Wilkins escorted the other two down the hall. As we watched them leave, I had a chance to notice the girl for the first time. Maggie, he had called her, was a short girl with a thick head of straight red hair. Her clothes and backpack had lots of purple accents, and I made a mental note that it was probably her favourite colour, in case we ended up becoming friends. She hadn't said anything to me directly, but she appeared like a kind person, and as I was deciding that I would make an effort to get to know her, I saw her look over her shoulder at us, silently crying for help with her eyes, but Max and I were powerless to do anything constructive, so I resolved to shrug my shoulders, as if to say "sorry you're stuck with her", before they turned a corner and disappeared our sight, finally giving me a chance to look over at my new homeroom partner.

Immediately, I was struck by his looks, he was a little bit taller and more built that me, but our frames were otherwise similar. His hair was short and it appeared to have been cut recently... not uncommon for a first day of school, but it looked somewhat natural, not overly stylized or gelled. His clothes seemed to fit him perfectly, which caught my eye for some reason, it's not that they looked crazy expensive or anything, but growing up in a world of bargain hunting and hand-me-downs, I wasn't used to seeing such well chosen clothes for someone my age. His teeth were sparkling white, but not obnoxiously so, and they appeared straight and proportional, unlike some of our contemporaries, who's mouths could be a source of absolute humiliation at our age. Most notable were his piercing blue eyes, glowing in stark contrast with his dark brown hair, they were mesmerizing, making him seem gentle and approachable. His over-all demeanour was unlike anything I'd seen before in a kid my age, he seemed confident, but not overly so, and that gave him and aura of coolness, but it didn't seem like he was aware of it, or that he cared for it, and for reasons unknown to me, I was driven to try to impress him right away, like I wanted him to like me, even though I didn't know anything about him yet. He spoke first:

Man, I'm glad we're not stuck with her, she looks mean... He said, nodding his head in the direction that Miss Wilkins had just left, His voice was smooth, and his tone was genuine.

Yeah, she looks like she should be in angry birds, haha. I joked cautiously, hoping it would land

A smile crept across his face, and a single dimple appeared on his right cheek, a sight which made me feel good, partly because his smile made me covet his attention and partly because I had caused that smile. I wasn't sure what was happening in my body, it was reacting oddly to this boy, the best I could come up with was that I had never really had a best friend but that I already wanted him to be it, the way he looked at me when I spoke felt like a warm blanket wrapped around my insides. Unsure of what to do next, I stared awkwardly at my feet and became overly-aware that I wasn't sure what to do with my hands, I tried to put them into my pockets to seem cool and nonchalant but it felt unnatural, and I could tell that he could tell, so I pulled them out and laid them at the sides of my thighs; a position that felt even more awkward than the last. Again, he broke the silence:

So where are you from anyways Freddy?

He remembered my name, a fact that should not have been surprising to me, seeing that he'd heard it three times in the last few minutes, but still, I felt special because he knew it. With new-found pride, I responded to his question.

Me and my mom just moved in from the country, I didn't really want to, but she got a new job in town so we had to move. I had left out some details...

they seemed too personal for a first encounter.

What about your dad? Did he stay back in the country? He asked innocently enough, unknowingly prodding at the details I was attempting to keep personal.

Shit. My dad had died just before the end of the school year. He worked at the sawmill and there had been an accident, leaving my mom alone to take care of us, the insurance had paid for our new house and the move, but there wasn't much left after that, so she had to get a better paying job to keep up with the bills. It wasn't something I really enjoyed discussing, but something about Max made me want to tell him, so, hesitantly, I broached the subject:

He... um... he died... that's why we moved here... A lump had formed in my throat mid-sentence, so the last part of my answer was more of a strained whisper

Oh shit, that's awful dude, sorry to hear about that. He put a hand on my shoulder, the look in his eye was sincere, and I could tell that he felt bad for bringing it up, and for some reason, I wanted to comfort him, but all I could say was

Thanks.

As the thoughts of my dad began to flood into

my head, I could feel my eyes welling up, I was ashamed that I was about to cry in front of this cool guy I hardly knew, but I was feeling overwhelmed and there didn't appear to be anything I could do about it. As a single tear made it's way down a familiar path on my cheek, his hand tightened a bit, and I could swear it felt like he was trying to take some of my pain, like maybe if we each took half of it, it wouldn't be so bad for either of us, and looking into his eyes, I could see hope and empathy, rather than the usual pity that I had grown accustomed to seeing when people found out my dad had died. I started to feel a little better, the warmth in his gaze filling me with comfort. The eye contact was intense, I felt like the world around us had disappeared, and it was having a healing effect on me, and just as he looked like he was about to speak, we were interrupted by the abrupt arrival of a lady who was substantially less put together than Miss Wilkins, and who was no doubt our tour guide for the day, Miss Friedman.

She clearly had not read the room before joining us and the way she entered it changed the vibe completely. It felt like we were watching a play, while she attempted to regain control of her environment. Her skin was dark and she had a natural radiance of beauty about her, though her hair was a little messy and her cardigan was buttoned up wrong. Even though she'd clearly been in a rush to get here, her energy appeared friendly, if not a little disorganized. Her purse hung off her elbow, as if it had fallen from her shoulder one too many times and she'd given up trying to put it back where it belonged, and she walked a little frantically as she approached the office door, but once she came in, she spoke to us and I could hear a thick Jamaican accent on her

I'm very sorry for being late gentlemen, please give me a moment to set down my things and I shall be with you right away.

Her voice was interesting, it had a lot of intonations for such a short sentence, and I enjoyed her choice of words, the way they sounded coming out of her mouth was almost melodic, like she was singing to us

Max looked at me and smiled a complicit smile, which I tried to return it as genuinely as possible, though my eyes were still a bit misty. We had just shared an intense moment together, like a secret that we were both in on, but we were both happy to be with Miss Friedman for the day, knowing that Tristan and Maggie were stuck with the bird lady.

As we walked down the halls, Miss Friedman highlighted various points of interest, but my focus was elsewhere. The moment I had just shared with Max was unlike any I had ever experienced before, it was almost as if we'd known each other for our whole lives and there was nothing about him that felt out of place. I looked over at him and he appeared to be paying close attention to every word that Miss Friedman was saying but during a pause in her speech, he quickly looked over at me, not to make eye contact, but just to ensure I was still there. I got the impression that he was checking in to make sure I was okay, and the thought made me feel good.

When lunchtime came, we joined back up with Tristan and Maggie in the cafeteria for a brief presentation on the rules of the campus. Then we sat and ate our lunches while Tristan went on and on about Miss Wilkins and how much of a bitch she was, but I wasn't paying much attention to him, I was still entranced by the intensity of Max's stare during our conversation, every time I closed my eyes, I could see his glowing blue eyes looking back at me and I searched for the meaning in my vision. After eating, we were all released to enjoy our weekends before the official start of the school year on Monday, but miss Friedman asked Max to stay behind to quickly do up some paperwork, so I left the school and stepped out into the late summer sun.

As I was waiting for my mother's car to come into view, Max caught up to me and grabbed at my forearm as he approached:

Hey Freddy, I'm glad I caught you...

I turned to face him, fearing that he would bring up my dead dad and make me want to cry all over again, but this time, out in public, so I awaited the rest of his sentence with a hint of reticence

...so what are you doing this weekend? He continued *You want to come to my house?*

Relieved that he wasn't rehashing our last conversation and surprised that he wanted to invite me over, I enthusiastically agreed, so he took down my phone number and told me that he would call once he had checked with his parents. My mom pulled up at that moment and true joy filled me as I got into the passenger's seat of her car and we drove home with her asking me a thousand questions about my new school and me mostly giving her one word answers, so that the rest of my brain power could continue to be devoted to thinking about Max and how I was going to get the chance to spend some time with him one-on-one.

After dinner, I was helping my mom clean up when the phone rang and my anticipation got the better of me, I dropped the cutlery I was washing and ran to pick up the receiver.

Hello? I asked, hopeful that it was Max

the voice on the other end sounded distant but familiar

Hello, is Freddy home? He hadn't recognized my voice. Being confused for my own mother on the phone was still the bane of my existence and a serious blow to my under-developed manhood.

Max? It's me, Freddy

Oh hey man! Sorry, you sound different on the phone... That was nice of him to say, but we both knew that was a lie... *So anyways, you still want to come over tomorrow? My mom says you can sleep over if you want!*

He sounded so hopeful, my heart was full at the thought that he wanted this friendship as much as I did.

Yeah! That sounds sick, but I have to check with my mom, hang on...

I set the phone down on the counter and ran into the dining room, where my mom was putting away the placemats, I explained the situation and began to beg her before she could even answer, but I knew that she would say yes, she was happy that I was making a friend, things had been hard for me this summer, and she was obviously relieved that I was appearing to be on the mend.

Okay... she said.... *But I want to speak with his parents first.*

I ran back to the kitchen and picked up the phone to tell Max the good news, and after our parents had spoken to each other, and all the details were squared away, my mom passed me back the phone and I heard Max grabbing the receiver back from his mom on the other end before finalizing the discussion

Sick man, I can't wait, I'll see you tomorrow.

Yeah dude, see you then!

We hung up and it hit me how quickly Max and I had bonded, the brief discussion we had earlier in the day had cemented something deep inside, and I think that the excitement of "belonging" overtook the both of us, it felt nice to be wanted.

I went to bed thinking about my new friend, but sleep did not come easily that night, the excitement of the next day kept me awake, like a child on Christmas Eve.

Max's house

◆ ◆ ◆

When I woke up, the sun was coming through my window and shining directly onto my duvet, heating up my bed, and giving me a reason to get up. I quickly showered and packed an overnight bag before heading down for breakfast with my mom, where I was lectured on etiquette when staying over at someone else's house. After agreeing to saying "please" and "thank you" at every opportunity and assuring her that I was going to chew with my mouth closed and keep my elbows off the table, my mom told me that it was time to leave, so I washed up my breakfast plate and made my way to the car outside.

We back out of the driveway from our modest bungalow and began to make our way towards the address that Max's mom had given us. The drive wasn't very long, but on it, I noticed the differences in neighbourhoods pretty quickly. The houses got bigger and bigger the farther we

got from our house and the lawns got more ornate and better manicured with each passing
one. We continued on with our journey until we
came into a neighbourhood with houses bigger
than I had ever seen, each one had a fence or a
wall surrounding it with a gate on the end of the
property, through the bars I could see shiny cars
in each driveway, all looking very expensive. We
pulled up to a gate with the numbers correspond-
ing to the ones on the small scrap of paper that
my mother had used to write down their address,
and my mom rolled down her window when she
stopped next to what appeared to be a speaker.
Without prompt, a voice came through asking

Mrs Miller? a woman's voice appeared in the
speaker

A little surprised, my mom responded

Um.. yes.... Unsure of what else to say

And with that, the gate opened up ahead of us,
allowing us to see the long road towards the
house that seemed really far away, the road was
lined on either side with apple trees, and beyond
them, a pristine lawn covered every inch of use-
able space that I could see. The car slowly made
its way down the road as we both took in the
grandiose view of the house we were nearing, it
looked like a beautiful castle and as we got closer,

it became clear that my initial assessment of its size was grossly underestimated. When we got to the house, we were greeted by Max and his mother, she was wearing a yellow sun dress and a large matching hat, looking almost regal yet somehow still modest, and I could tell she was wearing makeup, but it wasn't excessive, and her natural beauty didn't look like it needed much enhancing. She warmly invited us in and as we entered the house, I looked back at our pretty average sedan, thinking that it looked so out of place parked in front of this mansion, and I laughed at the contrast.

Upon walking in, I was struck by how normal everything looked, of course they had nice things, but none of them were gaudy or over the top, the house was arranged to be lived in by a family, and there wasn't as much art or ornate furniture as I was expecting based on the outside of the house.

Max's mom invited my mom to sit in the living room for some cold iced tea and Max and I each grabbed a glass as well, the day was still young but it was already quite hot and the promise of a cold drink was enticing. As our mothers made amicable chit chat, max tugged at my shirt and said

Come on, I want to show you around...

We set our empty glasses down on the coffee table and he led me further into the house.

We walked through the large dining room, with enough seating for a whole hockey team, and into a huge kitchen with a giant island and a great big window facing the back of the property. We continued on through a foyer and up a set of stairs onto a landing with three doors. Max pointed to the first one and said

That's the guest room.... His hand continued to move forward and he pointed to the second door saying.... *That's Tyler's room....* And without pointing, he made his way to the third door and said, with an air of pride... *and this is my room!*

He pushed open the door and inside, I could see what looked like an ordinary bedroom for a boy our age, but on a much bigger scale. An unmade queen size bed sat in the far corner, There was a pretty big TV with a video game console in another, and opposite that, there was a large desk with the usual amenities for doing homework, pencils, a calculator, a ruler and some papers strewn about. A pile of t-shirts and some socks laid near an opened laundry basket, clearly having missed their target, but for the most part, Max's room was clean, if not a little untidy.

As I made my way into his room and began to

examine the movie posters on the wall, Max instructed me to drop my overnight bag anywhere and he went to sit on his bed to watch me explore his room. I made my way in the direction of his desk and caught a glimpse of the papers that were on it. They had pencil drawings of cartoon superheroes and I thought they looked pretty good.

Did you make these? I asked, the way it came out, it was obvious that I was impressed.

Yeah, They're just some drawings I made, but they're not very good... He responded in false modesty.

I grabbed the stack to get a better look. Flipping through the pages, I could see that there was a theme to the images, a man in tights was seen beating up a bad guy, and then a crowd of people were cheering him on.

No way man, these are awesome! I reacted in honesty.

Aw, thanks man, I appreciate it. His humility was genuine.

I set down the papers and looked back at him,

So where's your parents bedroom? I posed the question because I'd realized that he'd pointed to all three doors on the floor and none of them had been his parent's room, which was confusing to me.

They sleep at the other end of the house, near the pool.

You have a pool? Perhaps, in my surprise, I had lost control of the volume of my voice and just about yelled, because he jumped slightly at my reaction. He laughed it off and asked

Yeah, you want to go for a swim?

I would, but I didn't bring a bathing suit... I was disappointed that he hadn't told me in advance, because it was already a pretty hot day and swimming sounded like a great idea, but without a bathing suit it would be impossible.

No problem dude, you can borrow one of mine! We're about the same size, so I'm sure I've got one that'll fit you.

He got up from his bed and made his way to his dresser, sliding open one of the bottom drawers and pulling out its contents until he came across a white and blue bathing suit that looked almost new. He tossed it in my direction.

Here you go, My mom bought me this one a little while ago, but it was a little too small for me, so I never wore it, it should fit you perfectly.

I held up the bathing suit and noticed that it still had the tags on it, he wasn't kidding, it had never been worn, but another concern came over me almost immediately,

Are we allowed?

To go swimming? He responded questioningly. *Of course we are, I just have to tell my mom!*

Reassured, I thanked him for the suit and we made our way downstairs, our moms were in the entrance hall and mine looked like she was getting ready to leave. She looked up as we entered the room and asked me to come over. As I approached, she pulled me in for a hug and told me to have fun, and then she put her head closer to mine and quietly whispered

I love you kiddo, be polite, don't embarrass me.

I was growing increasingly aware that our hug was dragging on and I was starting to feel embarrassed that I was hugging my mom for so long in front of my new friend, so, mildly annoyed, I whispered back

I love you too mom.... And began push her away lightly, so that she would get the message and let me go.

She looked a little hurt that I had pushed her off, but understood that she wasn't being cool, so she swallowed her pride and turned to leave, but not before giving me a look that served as a warning, and it was loud and clear to me that if I didn't behave, there would be hell to pay.

As the door closed, I turned back towards Max and his mom, staring at my feet, fully expecting to be harassed for hugging my mom for so long, but Max didn't really say anything about it, instead, he turned to his own mom and announced:

Mom, me and Freddy want to go swimming, is that okay?

Sure! She responded, and as we ran towards the back door, she yelled out. *But be safe!*

We walked outside and immediately, the heat hit us, it hadn't taken long for the day to get warm, and the humidity was hanging thick in the air. Max led me towards the side of the house and I noticed that I was carrying the bathing suit that he had lent me, but that he hadn't grabbed one in the process.

Aren't you gonna grab a bathing suit too?

Oh, mine's already in the changing shack. He responded.

As we turned the corner, I saw the pool deck enter my sights, I was a large bean shaped pool surrounded by massive natural looking patio stones, and at the far end stood a large rock wall that spanned the entire length of the pool and had a waterfall cascading into the shallow end. Max could tell that I was amazed at the sight, but he carried on around the left side of the pool and looked back before yelling:

Dude! You coming? Pulling me out of my stupor.

I wasn't really sure where he was leading me because the direction he was heading in seemed to end up funnelling into the rock wall, but as he approached it, he reached out his hand and turned a doorknob that I hadn't noticed and a door shaped hole appeared in the rock, into which he disappeared. Floored, I followed suit and made my way through the door and realized that the entire rock was actually what he had called their "changing shack" made to look like a cliff, and that inside was a well lit room with cubbies for each of the members of the house. A comfortable wooden bench sat in the middle and at the far end of the room was a giant open area with large shower heads all over and an opaque glass wall at the back, letting in a bunch of natural sunlight. Max threw me a towel from a stack and pointed to an empty cubby next to his where he told me I could leave my dry clothes while we swam. I held the towel and bathing suit, realizing that there didn't appear to be anywhere private to change and I immediately grew uncomfortable with the idea of undressing in front of my new friend, but in a spot of luck, Max stopped digging through his cubby and smacked himself on the forehead, exclaiming that he'd just remembered that his swimsuit had gone through the wash and that he had to go get it, so he ran out of the room, telling me that he'd be right back, leaving me alone in the giant change room to dress privately. I quickly undressed and slid on the swimsuit, not wanting Max to come back while I was naked and then spent a bit of time pulling at the price tag, which had yet to be removed from it. When I finally got it free and threw it in the nearby trashcan, I mad my way back out onto the pool deck, just as Max was coming back from his mission to the laundry room, swimsuit in hand.

Hey, I was right, that suit fits you perfectly... He said in passing, looking me up and down... *I'll only be a second.* He exclaimed, *don't go in without me.* With that, he ran into the change room and again I was left alone.

The sun was hot on my skin and I took the opportunity to take in my surroundings. All around the pool, small batches of matching patio furniture were arranged to divide the large open space. The pool itself had crystal blue water and I noticed that they didn't have a diving board or a slide like most of the pools I'd been to. The trees surrounding the deck area were far enough away that they didn't provide any unwanted shade, but a few long chairs were lined up with some closed parasols between them, presumably to avoid laying in the direct sun for too long. Just as I was thinking that I was getting quite hot and that I really wanted to get into the refreshing water, Max came out of the change room, sporting a red swimsuit and looking ready to swim.

I examined his body as he approached and was confused as to why I couldn't take my eyes off of it, as the sun shone on his skin, I searched him top to bottom for any imperfections, but could not find any. The muscles in his body seemed to dance as he walked and his skin looked so soft. I could tell that he spent a lot of time shirtless, because his chest, back and arms were darkened lightly by the sun with no distinguishable tan lines between them, and I began to feel envious of his physique and his life in general; he seemed to have it all, including a level of kindness that was unmatched by anyone I'd ever met before. He walked past me, evidently completely unaware of what was going on in my head and told me to follow him as he walked all the way around the outside of the pool, taking us to the other side of the rock wall where a staircase was hidden from sight if you were standing anywhere but directly in front of it.

We climbed the stairs and when we got to the top, now standing on the roof of the changing structure, max walked over to the edge closest to the pool and invited me to stand at his side. Looking down, a bout of fear came over me, we were about ten feet above the water and I'd never been great with heights. Max noticed my discomfort but tried to reassure me:

It's really deep at this end of the pool, I promise you won't get hurt. If you want we can jump together.

Without giving me any time to respond, he counted down from three, and when he reached one, I felt him grab my wrist tightly, probably so I wouldn't be able to back down, and then he jumped, pulling me forward and forcing me into a free fall.

I held my breath and closed my eyes out of fear, my stomach was in my throat, but the fall was kind of exhilarating. My feet hit the surface of the water, and before I knew it it was over, and I was deep underwater, opening my eyes to try to get my bearings. Max had released my wrist, but he was only two or three feet away from me and I could see him watching me struggle with reality, grinning from ear to ear.

As we resurfaced, max wiped the water from his face with his hand and waited for me to react to what had just happened. I was a little angry that he hadn't consulted me before pulling me over the edge, or that he hadn't even given me a chance to think about it, but looking over at his smile, it was hard to hold on to my anger, and I playfully splashed some water into his face.

You jerk I said, trying to sound semi-serious.

But he just laughed it off.

Would you have jumped if I hadn't pulled you in?

I thought about it for a brief moment...*Probably not...* I had to admit

Then I'm glad I did it. Was his only response before turning and swimming away from me.

I was left with the realization that I'd just faced a fear because of Max, and we both knew that I was the better for it, but it didn't seem like he wanted any recognition for pushing me to expand my boundaries, he just appeared happy that I had tried something different and that I didn't hate it. The more I thought about it, the more I had to admit to myself that jumping off the rock had actually been kind of fun and that despite having feared it just a moment ago, I wanted to do it again. I began to swim to the edge of the pool, and as I pulled myself out, and made my way towards the stairs, I looked over my shoulder to see genuine surprise in Max's face as he watched me heading back for more. He didn't hesitate to follow me and soon, we were both standing at the edge of the rock, ready to take the leap again.

Do you want to do it together again? He asked, searching my face for the answer.

Sure. I responded, my initial confidence wavering between the time I left the pool and now, standing at the edge.

Again, he could sense my reticence, so he grabbed my hand, interlacing his fingers with mine, he knew I needed the encouragement, but that he wouldn't have to physically pull me in again. His hand surprised me when it touched mine, it was soft and warm, and somewhat familiar. I looked at his face, searching for meaning in his hand holding, but his genuine smile and joyful eyes just told me that he was happy in this moment, there was no thought behind it, it was just something that he did because it felt right. And then he counted down again, and in a moment of bravado and revenge, I jumped in before the "go" and this time, I was the one to pull him in.

As we resurfaced, our roles were reversed, I was watching his face, anticipating his reaction, and with a coy smile, he splashed some water at my face and called me a jerk. Wiping the water from my face, I splashed him back and this commenced an epic splash fight that ended in him chasing me around the pool, until he caught up to me and dunked my head under water. Upon freeing myself, I resurfaced and yelled out playfully:

Oh, you're gonna pay for that.

Prompting him to escape past my arm's reach before I could grab him, at which point, he swam away frantically and I gave chase.

Our games continued on for a while before his mom popped he head out through a large window and announced that it was time for lunch and that we should get changed before coming in.

A little out of breath, Max and I agreed that we'd had enough swimming for now and began to swim back to the edge of the pool closest to the door of the change room. We both got out and made our way back into the big open room, where Max grabbed his towel and threw me mine before walking past me to the back of the room where the shower heads lined the walls. We hung both towels up on a bar by the entrance and he approached a control pad with a bunch of dials and buttons on it, pressing a few of them, making two of the shower heads, side by side in a corner of the room, come alive with falling water.

I followed his lead and made my way to one of the shower streams, where the water hitting my body was at the perfect temperature, not too hot or too cold, when Max reached over to pick up a bottle of body wash from a shelf that was built into the shower wall. He squeezed some in his hand and handed me the bottle, before working the soap into his hair and letting the bubbles wash away the chlorine from the pool. I was mesmerized, watching the foam trail down his body, making its way through all the nooks and crannies of his torso, before running down the outside of his bathing suit and landing at his feet on its way to the drain in the middle of the floor.

I couldn't recall having ever watched someone else shower before and the whole experience seemed foreign to me. I was hyper-aware that I was witnessing what is normally a very private ritual and I was a little self conscious that he was about to see me doing the same. With my eyes still traveling all over his body, I remembered that I was holding the bottle of soap and I thought I'd better snap out of my current state before Max noticed that I was staring at him. I didn't want him to feel awkward, so I squeezed some soap into my own hand and began to emulate Max's moves, working the shower gel into my hair and letting gravity take the suds to the drain.

It felt a little odd showering next to someone else, but Max seemed completely comfortable with it and he gave me another look, with no evident thought behind it, just his accepting eyes and comforting smile, assuring me that there was nothing wrong with this situation, and that any anxiety I had around him was imaginary and un-founded.

We finished showering and dried off, I wrapped my towel around my waist before changing under the cover of the fabric. We got dressed and went back into the house, where the air conditioning felt good on my skin and his mother had set out two plates at the table, each with a grilled cheese cut diagonally and a hand full of chips. In the centre of the table was the large glass pitcher of lemonade refilled with fresh slices of lemon float-ing around, and the condensation running down the side was calling to me with the promise of the cool refreshing drink inside. Max served us each a glass and we both gulped them down without stopping to breathe.

As we ate, the sky outside began to change quickly and soon, light drops of rain began tap-ping on the large window in the kitchen. Max and I ate in silence, occasionally looking over at one another and sharing a complicit smile. We knew next to nothing about each other, and yet it did not seem like we needed to speak, his face told me that nothing I could say would make him think any less of me, and I felt like he could do no wrong; I was beginning to feel confident in think-ing that we were becoming friends, but I wasn't sure if he felt the same way.

After lunch, the rain had begun to come down

with more vigour and Max asked if I wanted to play video games in his room while we waited out the weather. I didn't really care what we did, as long as we were spending time together, so I agreed, and after cleaning up from our lunch, we made our way back up the stair into his room, where Max turned on his TV and powered up his console so we could play his favourite two person racing game.

Video games were not my strong suit so it took a lot of effort to not lose by too much, but I could tell that he caught on, because near the middle of our third race, he began to lag intentionally, giving me a chance to catch up. Right before crossing the finish line, I witnessed his car make a sudden right turn and hit the track wall, and he appeared to spend more than a reasonable amount of time trying to get it facing in the right direction again, giving me the opportunity to pass him and finish the race in first place. He pretended to be angry about the loss for a brief moment but then his attention turned to me and he patted me on the back in congratulations.

Good job dude, you won fair and square. He lied

Thanks, I guess I got lucky. I responded, playing along.

The victory itself felt hollow, I knew he'd let me win, but the fact that he'd made an effort for it to seem like an accident, felt amazing, I could tell that he really cared about my feelings, and it felt good to have someone who wanted me to be happy.

The afternoon wore on, with more video games and laughter, but the rain never let up, so after dinner, when darkness began to set in, we settled down to watch a movie. Max had set up some pillows and sleeping bags on the ground for us to get comfortable, and before we sat down, we agreed that we should get ready for bed, in case we fell asleep.

The movie started, but I wasn't paying too much attention to it, instead, I sat in silence, with thoughts of the day running through my head. I wondered why Max and I had gotten so close, so quickly. I knew that I wanted him to like me, because he was so much cooler than me in every way, but I could not figure out why he wanted to be my friend, so far I had just presented myself as a cry-baby who was scared of heights and who sucked at video games. I wondered what had compelled him to hold my hand earlier, It was not something I thought most people did with their friends, or at least it wasn't something I had ever done with a friend before. I found myself in this amazing house, with a guy who was way too cool for me, and all of a sudden, I started to feel really out of place; this was not my life, I didn't hang out with rich people, I didn't swim in private pools, I didn't make friends easily, especially not without having something to offer in return. My thoughts turned to anxiety and I started to feel really uncomfortable, and I was beginning to think that I wanted to go home, back to my regular bungalow, with our modest sedan in the driveway, back to my mom who didn't need to ask me any questions to understand how I was feeling, back to my comfort.

I must have been breathing heavily, because Max looked over at me with a hint of concern in his face, he looked into my eyes and placed his soft hand on my shoulder again, like he'd done the day before when I told him about my dad.

Is everything okay?

I hesitated before responding, how could I explain that I wanted to go home, if he didn't think I was a wuss already, he certainly would after calling off a sleep over because I "missed my mommy". Overwhelmed and unsure what to say, my emotions got the better of me and my eyes began to well up again, I turned away from him so he wouldn't see me cry.

Hey, what's the matter? The concern was growing in his voice. *It's okay man, whatever it is, you can tell me.* He said reassuringly.

As he spoke, his hand migrated to the back of my shoulder and he began to rub my back lightly, I could tell that even though he didn't quite understand the problem, he wanted desperately to make it better. His empathy was powerful and the physical contact began to have a soothing affect on me. Immediately, I started to feel ridiculous for the thoughts I'd been having, Max had been nothing but nice to me, and I was questioning his intentions. It was obvious that he was genuine and that his actions spoke for him, he was a really good person and for some reason, he wanted to be my friend, and that should have been good enough for me, but despite that reasoning, I heard myself say

Max, you're so cool, why in the hell are you being so nice to me? It sounded harsh coming out of my mouth, and immediately I regretted the way I'd said it.

What do you mean Freddy? He asked, seeming unfazed by my tone.

Well, it's just that you're this really cool guy, with all this money, and you're really nice, and it's probably not very hard for you to make friends, so why are you wasting your time with me? I'm just a regular guy, I cry a lot, I'm scared of pretty much everything and I don't really have much to offer.

This time, I sounded pathetic.

He laughed, *What do you mean? You're funny, like remember when you said Miss Wilkins looked like an angry bird? Umm... you're honest, like how you told me all that stuff about your dad, and plus, I could tell right away when I met you that you're a good person...* He paused briefly, as if he were looking for the right way to say the next part... *there's just something about you that makes me want to be your friend...* He said very sincerely, all the while still rubbing my back.

That word had caught my attention, "friend", I needed him to clarify

So are you saying that we're friends? I asked tentatively, turning over slightly to see if he was telling the truth

He seemed surprised by my question.

Of course we're friends, I wouldn't have invited you over if I didn't think we were. He responded reassuringly, almost scoffing at my ridiculous question.

I put my head down, feeling ashamed that I'd been such a baby about the whole thing.

You mean that?

Look at me... He ordered, so I lifted my head slightly, he waited for my gaze to meet his... *I mean that.* He finished.

He followed that statement of fact with another

smile, erasing all of my doubts about him, his dimple told me that he was telling the truth and I was relieved that he saw value in me. Without speaking, he settled back into his pillow, contented that the moment had passed and we continued to watch the movie silently, both assured that we'd officially become friends. I followed suit and relaxed into my bed, light hearted and filled with joy, soon, sleep gently took me into a land of dreams, where Max and I fought bad guys together and were cheered on by a whole city.

Sunday

◆ ◆ ◆

When I woke up, The sun was coming in through the window and shining directly in my face. I looked over at the clock and realized it was early for a Sunday, but I didn't feel tired anymore, so I thought I'd just lay there and enjoy the quiet for a bit. I looked over and Max was still sleeping on his stomach with his head facing me, his sleeping bag had been pushed down to his torso, he must have gotten hot in the night. The sun was bouncing off the skin on his back and I watched it rise and fall as he breathed calmly. The look on his face could best be described as satisfied, telling me that he must be having a good dream. I was beginning to grow accustomed to that look, it seemed like he was always smiling, and always trying to make me do the same. He stirred a bit and I heard him inhale deeply as his eyes began to open, he noticed that I was staring and his smile grew bigger.

Hey, how'd you sleep? He asked, but I could tell the

the real question he wanted to ask was whether or not I was feeling okay after last night's talk.

Great, thanks... I wanted him to know that my fears from last night had passed and that

I was happy I'd slept over, but I wasn't sure how to say it, so instead I continued with...*This pillow is really comfortable.*

He acknowledged my response with a little laugh, and despite having said nothing, I could see that he was relieved that I'd slept well, satisfied with my answer, he changed the subject: *Man, you sure do snore loud.* He jabbed lightly

What? I responded, jokingly incredulous. *I do not snore!* I laughed and poked him back, my finger landing in his rib, causing him to jump... I guess he was ticklish.

His mouth slightly agape in disbelief that I'd found a weakness of his, he pulled his arms in tightly to prevent another assault, but determined to exploit my new found power over him, I leapt on top of him and began trying to separate his arm from his side to expose his ticklish area. He struggled against me, and being stronger, he managed to turn himself around, pushing me off him and taking his turn sitting on top of me to see if I was also susceptible to being tickled. Horrified that he'd managed to turn the tables on me,

I fought to keep him from finding any weaknesses in my armour, but unfortunately, he managed to burrow his fingers into my armpits and made me squirm to try to escape his grasp. I laughed involuntarily and yelled for him to stop, but he just kept moving his fingers around, extending my torture.

STOP! STOP! I'M GONNA PEE EVERYWHERE IF YOU DON'T STOP! I yelled in desperation.

Unsure of whether or not I was telling the truth, but unwilling to deal with the consequences if I was being honest, he released me from his grip and got off me to let me go, he extended his hand to help me to my feet and I grabbed it to heave myself up, but when I reached my feet, I pulled his hand up, leaving his ribs wide open, and with my free hand, I dug into his ribs quickly, making him laugh and wither. Again, he managed to get hold of the situation quite quickly and before I knew it, he had both my arm locked at my side, with his arms wrapped around me tightly to prevent any further attacks. I fought a little to get free, but realizing that I was outmatched, I opted for an apology instead, hoping my words might be stronger than my muscles.

Haha, sorry, I couldn't resist... but seriously, if you don't let me go, I'm going to pee in my pants. The urgency in my voice was sincere.

How do I know this isn't another trick? He asked, sceptically

I promise, cross my heart... anyways, if I try again, you'll just have me in a headlock right away or something, you're much faster and stronger than me... I tried to appeal to his ego, my need to pee was becoming a bit of a concern

Hmmm.... I guess you're right. He relented, and then he added in false bravado: *I am pretty strong...*

We both laughed, and he released me again, this time, I had no desire to lose another fight, I really needed to pee, so I went to the washroom, leaving him to bask in the glory of his victory.

When I came back into the room, he was already dressed and he told me to change out of my pyjamas so we could go have breakfast. I quickly pulled on some shorts and a different t-shirt and we made our way down the stairs towards the kitchen.

When we walked in, there was a man sitting at the kitchen island sipping a cup of coffee and reading a newspaper, he was so focused that he didn't hear us come in, but from beside me, I heard Max yell out:

DAD!

And then he ran up and hugged him deeply as his dad struggled to set down his cup of coffee so as not to spill any on himself. He smiled a familiar smile, one that he obviously shared with his son and laughed a little as he responded.

Hi kiddo, I missed you. His voice was deep and I could sense warmth in it, my first impression of him was that he seemed really nice.

When did you get in? Where's Tyler? Max asked excitedly.

Again, his father laughed as he tried to peel Max off of him so he could look at his face.

We got in late last night, Tyler's sleeping, it was a long drive, I don't think he'll be up for a while.

I still stood at the door frame, realizing that I was witnessing a sweet moment between a father and son who were being reunited for the first time in a while. It dawned on me that I had never bothered to ask Max about his dad, even though I'd had many opportunities, and I felt a little guilty about having made the entire weekend about myself so far. As I contemplated making a bigger effort to be a better friend to Max by focusing on him more often, I heard his dad ask in a friendly tone

And who's this? He was looking at me, but it

felt like he was asking us both the question, so Max jumped in.

Oh right! Dad, this is my friend Freddy, he's gonna go to the same school as me, we met at orientation. An air of pride was audible in his voice when he called me his friend, Like he was showing me off, and it made me feel special.

Freddy, eh? He got up from his stool and walked over to me to extend his hand. *Well hi Freddy, it's very nice to meet you.*

I held out my hand and he grabbed it firmly, but not too hard. As he shook it, he looked me right in the eyes and I saw the same warmth that I'd noticed so often in Max's stare.

It very nice to meet you, Mr. Longview. I said, trying to sound as polite as possible, I could practically hear my mother's voice in the back of my head giving me orders.

He laughed

Mr. Longview was my father, you can call me Scott. He was smiling, but I could tell that he was being serious, and not wanting to insult him, I tried again

It's very nice to meet you... I paused, unsure If what I was about to say was going to get me in trouble...

Scott...

That's better! He put a hand on my shoulder to put me at ease, and when he saw me sigh in relief, he changed the subject. *C'mon, are you boys hungry? Your mom made some chocolate chip pancakes before she went to the grocery store this morning, I'm just keeping them warm in the oven.*

And without waiting for a response, he made his way to the oven and pulled out a large metal tray with a pile of pancakes on it. He grabbed some plates from the cupboard and forks from the drawer, placing them side by side on the kitchen island, telling Max and I to sit down, and then he put the entire tray in front of us, with instructions

Serve yourself boys, eat as much as you want, but just make sure there's enough left or Tyler when he wakes up.

Max gave his father a deliberate head nod, indicating that we'd understood, and then he reached over and put a pancake on my plate before serving himself.

As we ate, I looked over at Max and I could tell that having his dad home had put him in an even better mood. I had a question bouncing around in my head, but I didn't want to look stupid asking it, so I subtly leaned over to Max and asked in a low tone of voice:

Hey, who's Tyler?

Max seemed surprised, it hadn't dawned on him that he and his dad had been talking about this Tyler guy without giving me any context, but I could see that realization hitting him now.

Tyler's my big brother. He spoke with pride. *Him and my dad have been away on a fishing trip for a few weeks, you're gonna love him, he's the best!* Clearly max was excited to see his brother.

"The best" he had said, I thought Max was the best, but after meeting his dad, it wasn't hard for me to imagine that his brother was probably fairly similar, the whole family had been so nice to me. Max's energy was contagious and even I was getting excited for Tyler to wake up.

After we'd stuffed our faces with pancakes, and our bellies were quite full, we put our dirty dishes in the dishwasher and Max told me he wanted to show me something outside. We put our shoes on and stepped out into the cool morning air, but not before Max told his dad that we'd be out back, to which his dad yelled back

Okay boys, have fun but be safe.

I followed Max as he led me towards the wall

that ran all the way around his property, and at the very back corner, a gate separated his yard from a forest. We walked through the gate and made our way down a path that took us into the woods. A few hundred feet in, Max stopped in front of a large tree and turned around to face me, but he didn't say a word, instead, he waited for me to speak, as if he knew what question I was going to ask him.

Where are we going dude?

He didn't reply, instead he simply pointed up with his finger, directing me to look up into the tree, about twenty feet up, I could see a platform that sat in a crotch between three large branches. I looked back at his face in disbelief, I'd never actually seen a real tree house before, at least not one outside of a movie, and excited I asked:

Can we go up?

Yeah, follow me. He was glowing, evidently happy that I thought it was as cool as he'd hoped.

We walked around to the backside of the tree where some pieces of lumber were nailed to the trunk, making a sort of ladder for climbing. Again, Max led the way and climbed up really quickly, I followed behind, taking a little longer, but when I got up to the platform, he was already sitting on the ground in the middle, waiting for me to arrive.

He seemed a little surprised that I'd made it up so quickly.

Aren't you scared to be up here? He asked hesitantly, I could tell that he didn't want to bring it up, in case I hadn't realized how high up we were yet, but his curiosity got the better of him.

Not if we're not gonna jump off... I responded... *Plus, you're up here too, so it's gotta be safe right?*

Max nodded his head in agreement while I began to take in my surroundings.

There wasn't much to it, just a floor about ten feet by ten feet, some railing surrounded the entire thing to prevent anyone from falling off, and the only opening was where I stood, at the top of the ladder. I sat in front of Max and looked around in awe; though it didn't seem like much, the tree house felt so cool. In the movies, tree houses were always like a symbol of freedom, it was a place where kids could go to get away from adults. I was extremely envious of him at this point.

Is it yours? Did you build this?

I found it when we moved into the house. My dad checked it out and he said that it was solid, so he lets me come up here whenever I want. He said that next summer, he's gonna help me fix it up even better, with a roof and some walls, and he'll even let me camp out here when it's done!

Woah man, that's so cool! My awe came through in my voice.

A coy smile crept across his face... *wait though, you haven't even seen the best part yet.*

Confused, I watched him turn his attention to some floorboards near his right hand. He slid his fingers into the gap and removed one of them, reaching down into the hole and pulling out a large ziplock bag with what looked like a magazine inside it. When he got it out of the bag, I realized that it was a comic book with a creepy looking monster on the cover, holding a sword in one hand and a severed human head in the other. He handed me the book and I quickly flipped through the pages, seeing depictions of gory battles with blood and guts on just about every page, before I landed on a page where the monster was ripping the face off of an enemy while he begged for his life amid screams of pain. You could see the muscles and bones being exposed as the skin was being peeled off, and his eyeballs were bulging out.

I had never seen anything like this, it was both gruesome and amazing, the drawings looked so detailed, they were clearly out of a disturbed person's imagination. In my house, I would never have been allowed to keep something so senselessly violent.

This is sick! Your parents let you have this?

No way man, if they knew this was here, they would have thrown it out a long time ago.

Well then how did you get this?

Tyler bought it for me when he went to New York last year on a school trip.

This is so gross. I said, pointing to the picture of the guy having his face ripped off.

Yeah, I love that one, but check this one out... Max pulled the comic book gently out of my hands and flipped forward a few pages before finding the one he was looking for and turning it back towards me so I could see the image.

The full page picture showed the monster standing on a pile of dead bodies behind a woman, his arms wrapped around her torso, burying his face into her neck, and you could clearly see that she was enjoying it. The most striking thing about this image however was her body, she was hardly wearing any clothing, just a small pair of tight briefs on her lower half and a loose sleeveless shirt that was being pulled slightly sideways by the monster's hug, exposing the side of her breast and I could make out small bumps in the front of her shirt where her nipples would be. I was baffled by the image, I'd never seen a half naked woman being depicted this way before. There was something sexual about the picture and looking at it felt somehow good but wrong at the same time, making my stomach fill with butterflies.

Cool huh? Max asked, beaming with pride

Uhuh. Was all I could muster as I nodded my head, unable to take my eyes off the picture.

Just then, we faintly heard his mom's voice, yelling from the house.

Boys, time to come in, Freddy's mom will be here in a few minutes.

Max and I scrambled to put the comic back, as if we'd been caught, and we collected ourselves before climbing down and running back up the path towards his yard. We went straight up to his room and he sat on his bed while I packed my bag back for the return home. Max watched me put my things away and for the first time since I'd met him, a look of sadness came over his face.

I wish you didn't have to leave, I had a lot of fun with you.

I don't think he could have possibly known what

effect those words had on me, hearing that he wanted me to stay longer felt like I had won the lottery.

I'm bummed too, but at least we'll get to see each other tomorrow at school. I said, trying to cheer him up.

He clearly hadn't thought about that, because it seemed to hit him like a revelation, and the smile I'd grown so accustomed to had made it's way back onto his face in no time.

Oh yeah! I forgot... I can't wait!

With that, we heard the front door open and a friendly greeting coming up from the main entrance, announcing that my mom had arrived, so Max and I started to leave his room, as we stepped into the hallway, we were met by an older looking guy who was clearly just getting out of bed, and I surmised that this must be Tyler, Max's older brother. His hair was a mess and he was wearing basketball shorts and a T-shirt that had had the sleeves ripped off of it, exposing his muscular arms and parts of his ribs, chest and back, which all seemed equally muscular. His face had a slight five-o -clock shadow to it and his eyes, though still somewhat glued together by sleep, were as blue as Max's and his dad's. He looked to be about eighteen years old, and without even hearing him speak, I could tell why Max looked to him with such admiration. He noticed us standing there and I saw his dimple emerge as Max ran up and hugged him hard, like he'd done to his father earlier in the day.

TYLER! His voice squeaked in excitement.

Hey kiddo, how you been? Tyler responded through giggles at how ridiculous his brother was being

I missed you! Was Max's response.

Tyler hugged his brother back and then they released each other, Max took a step back and stood at my side as Tyler turned his attention to me and the smile left his face.

Tyler, this is my friend Freddy, Freddy, this is Tyler.

Tyler looked me up and down, looking very serious, I could feel him judging me, seeing if I was good enough to be friends with his only sibling.

Freddy, eh? He walked in closer to me, as he released the smile that he was clearly holding back, trying to make me think he might not approve. *Any friend of Max's must be cool.* He finished, chuckling at my sight of relief, clearly pleased with himself that he'd convinced me that I might not pass his test.

He reached out and tussled my hair and spoke

again. *It's nice to meet you Freddy.*

It's nice to meet you too. I managed to squeak out, still a little shaken by Tyler's game.

From downstairs, we heard their mom calling up

Max, Freddy's mom is here.

I looked back at Tyler, and he gave me an approving smile and patted me on the back as Max and I left him to his morning ritual. We walked down the stairs and I was greeted by my mom, who was clearly making an effort not to hug me for too long when I came to say hi. We said our goodbyes and Max followed us out to the door as we walked towards my mom's car. Just before I got in, Max hollered out from his post at the door jamb:

Bye Freddy, see you at school tomorrow.

And I replied, *Yeah man, see you then.*

My mom and I got in the car and began our journey back through the rich neighbourhood towards our house so I could prepare for the real first day of school.

The (real) first day of school

❖ ❖ ❖

My mom dropped me off at the front gates of the school early in the morning and I made my way out of the car, assuring her that I'd have a good day. I walked through the gate and into the school yard, where the hustle and bustle of the first day had already begun. All around me, kids were standing in small groups talking and laughing, presumably catching up on a summer's worth of stories and gossip. I carefully wandered through the crowd, looking for a familiar face, all the while making sure not to misstep and make a bad first impression by accidentally running into someone or stepping on a future classmate's new shoes or something. Off in the distance, I spotted Tristan monologging to a small crowd of people who appeared to be very interested in what he was saying, but I opted not to call out to him, because I didn't want to be stuck listening to him talk for the rest of the morning.

A soft hand came to rest on my shoulder and I turned to see Maggie standing behind me, looking somewhat relieved that she'd found a friendly face in the sea of strangers. I had to admit that seeing her familiar long strawberry hair and her freckled nose in the endless crowd of anonymous faces felt like I had found a life raft to cling onto.

Hey, you're Freddy, right? She appeared a little overwhelmed by the chaos around us.

Yeah, and your name is Maggie?

She breathed a sigh of relief that she was no longer alone in the crowd, and acknowledged my question with a head nod and a smile.

Holy cow, It's crazy here this morning, this is a lot of people. She said, looking around at all the other kids.

Yeah, but they all seem nice enough. I answered, trying to comfort her and myself at the same time.

Have you seen the others yet? She asked, referring to Max and Tristan.

Well, Tristan is over there,.. I pointed to the circle that had formed around Tristan, She rolled her eyes, clearly she'd gotten the same impression of him that I had... *And I haven't seen Max yet this morning.*

Just then, Max walked up, seeming amused by the insanity of the first day of school.

Hey guys, am I ever glad I found you two, this place is nuts. He said, looking around.

I noticed something in Maggie change when Max walked up, her face tuned red and she tilted her head down slightly, as if she didn't want to look directly at him. She acknowledged his statement with a simple *Mhm.* And began to fiddle with her backpack straps. It was very strange behaviour, but I chalked it up to first day jitters.

Max turned his attention to me:

Hey, so Tyler brought me another comic book, I guess they stopped over in some town on the way back and he managed to hide it from my dad, you have to come see it, it's even grosser than the other one. His excitement was palpable, and somewhat contagious.

That sounds awesome, I can't wait. I really had wanted to be invited over again, Max's house was the best.

Maggie looked annoyed that she wasn't in on whatever we were talking about, but she brushed it off, and then a bell rang and all of the students in the schoolyard looked up towards the building, disappointed that their socializing time had passed. They all walked over to a door and began filing in, being directed by teachers towards the auditorium. Max, Maggie and I opted to follow suit and pushed our way through the herd, all the while making sure not to lose track of each other so we could sit together during the assembly.

Walking into the large room, the sound of other kids talking and laughing was filling the space from wall to wall. A set of stairs went along either side of the rows of seating, heading all the way up to the very back of the room like a movie theatre. At the front of the room was a large stage with a black curtain on three sides, defining the space around a row of chairs which were set up along the hardwood floor behind a podium with the schools emblem on the front. Max, Maggie and I found three empty seats in the middle of a row and we apologized and shuffled our way towards them. Max was ahead, and he sat in the middle of the three so Maggie and I were forced to sit on either side of him, I was happy that he had done so, because I really wanted to sit next to him.

When we finally settled in, I looked around at the faces of the kids I hadn't met yet and they all seemed fairly friendly. None of them were staring us down, they all seemed preoccupied by their respective groups of friends, and my initial fears about being hunted down as the new kid were somewhat alleviated, I was happy that no one seemed to care about me.

A group of seven boys filed into the auditorium and made their way up the stairs to the back, I watched them as they found an entire empty row at the very top, as if it had been reserved for them. In their midst, I saw Tristan being lead by an equally tall kid who had his arm around his shoulder, it looked like they were eyeballing the crowd and the tall boy was pointing out some of the kids in the room and giving Tristan small tid-bits of information about each one. The vibe I got from the group was that they were the cool kids and that Tristan was being inducted into their circle.

As I was investigating Tristan's new friends, a noise caught my attention at the front of the room and made me turn around, only to realize that all the chairs on the stage were now filled with faculty and a stocky, balding man wearing a brown suit was standing behind the podium, trying to get the microphone to work. After a bit of screeching and popping, his voice finally came through over the large speakers that were placed strategically throughout the room.

Hello? Hello? Hello ladies and gentlemen, please

quiet down and take your seats... He waited a moment for the room to calm down.... *Hello everyone, as you know, my
name is Principal Newridge, and I just want to welcome you all to a new year at Mount Trinity Middle
School...*

He paused for a moment, presumably expecting applause, but the only clapping we heard came from behind him, in the row of teachers. Upon closer inspection, I noticed that the clapping was coming from Miss Wilkins, who was sitting at the far end of the row, she slowed her clapping and stopped completely when she realized she was the only one doing it, but she didn't seem embarrassed, instead, she gave the entire room a stern look for not joining her...

Thank you miss Wilkins... He continued... *Anyways, so a few points of order for this morning, number one, there have been some staffing changes, Miss Klein will no longer be with us, so Miss Wilkins will be taking her place as vice principal...* Again, he paused for a reaction but none came, so he continued... *And we have a new gym teacher this year, everyone, please give a warm welcome to Mister Fowler.*

He turned and pointed to a younger muscular man sitting in the middle of the row, he stood up and gave everyone a wave and it was immediately noticeable that he was in good shape.

His hair was well groomed and he had a friendly smile, so the crowd reacted in kind and gave him an enthusiastic cheer before he sat back down.

Settle down, settle down... continued Principal Newridge... *Okay, number two, after a few incidents last spring, the school board has decided that students will no longer be allowed to ride skateboards on school property...*

A loud groan of disbelief came from behind me and when I turned to see it's source, I was unsurprised to find that it was coming from the group of cool looking boys that I saw walking in with Tristan.

That's enough gentlemen... The comment was directed at the back row of the auditorium... *Okay, and finally, your student body president, Hellen Birch, has an announcement.*

A loud "woo" came from the guys in the back row, and Principal Newridge shot a disapproving look their way as a blond girl stood up from her chair in the front row, and made her way up onto the stage and to the podium. From far away, it was hard to distinguish her features, but it was evident that she was very good looking and her choice of tight clothes were accentuating her body's curves, it became obvious that the "woo" coming from the back of the room had been meant inappropriately to announce that they thought this girl was hot. When she got to the microphone and spoke, her voice sounded soft and petite.

Thank you Principal Newridge... She paused and looked back as he took his place in the row of chairs behind the podium. When he had taken his place and acknowledged her thanks, she turned back to the room and continued her speech... *As you know, the beginning of the year means that it's already time for our first fundraiser, so we will be holding the harvest dance at the end of next week.* She paused slightly, waiting for the chatter and cheers to subside from the room at the mention of a dance. *tickets are going to be available at the front office and the library and they will be five dollars each. Please come everyone, it's going to be a really fun dance and the student council needs the funds.*

The news of a dance seemed to be well received because the low chatter which filled the room never really died down completely for the end of her speech, I turned to ask Max and Maggie if they were planning on going to the dance and I noticed Maggie staring at Max looking hopeful, I couldn't quite figure out what she was hoping to get from him, but before too long, I got my answer when she spoke up before I had the chance

Hey Max, do you think you're gonna go to the dance?

Max seemed surprised at the question, but he turned to me before answering, searching my face for any clues about whether or not I thought it was a good idea

What do you think Freddy? Max asked

I was a little stunned, but I tried to play it off cool... *Who knows, it could be fun...* I said, as nonchalantly as possible.

With that, Max turned back to Maggie and cheerfully answered her original question... *Yeah, hey, we should all go together!...* He continued

A slight hint of disappointment was visible in Maggie's face, it obviously wasn't the answer she was hoping for, but she sucked it up and replied... *Cool, that will be fun...* I could tell that she was trying to sound as sincere as possible.

Principal Newridge came back onto the microphone and dismissed us for the day, sending us to our homerooms, so Maggie was forced to leave us and head to her own class, leaving Max and I to exit the auditorium together and begin our walk towards our first class of the day.

When we got to our homeroom, we realized that we were some of the last to arrive and most of the other students in our class had already found seats. At the very back of the class, I recognized three of the boys from the group that had been heckling during the assembly. The tall one was sitting between two stockier boys and the three of them seemed to be snickering about something together. Max and I found two empty seats next to each other in the front row and sat down while we waited for Miss Friedman to come in and start the class. As we set down our bags and finally looked up towards the chalkboard at the front, we saw that someone had drawn a crude picture of a stick figure with the words "Principal N" above it's head and a giant penis pointed directly at his face, and based on the snickering coming from the back row, the culprits would not be hard to identify.

When she finally entered the room, Miss Friedman went straight for the drawing and erased it vigorously with the sleeve of her shirt, turning back to the class with a disapproving scowl aimed directly at the now quiet boys in the back row. Satisfied that she had made her point clear to the perpetrators, she turned to the rest of the class and began her day as if nothing had happened.

Good morning students, as you know, I am Miss Friedman and this will be your homeroom for the semester. I will be assigning you seats in alphabetical order, and I expect you to adhere to them with-

out complaint

An incredulous sight was heard from the back row, which Miss Friedman ignored.

She started walking from one desk to another, naming the student that would be occupying it, and the others in the class began to collect their things for the move to their designated locations. That is how I learned the names of the three boys who were in the troublesome pack that had been causing such a stir all morning.

The tall one who appeared to be the leader was Dylan Eaton, and he didn't seem too pleased with his seat near the front of the class.

His two goons were Harold Riggles and Philip Scarlet, who were both much happier to find that they were seated next to each other, a point which they made clear by high-fiving loudly at the news, but not before correcting Miss Friedman on their preferred names, Big-Rig and Scar, which were evidently nicknames that they were proud of.

Max and I were separated by a short skinny boy named Nathaniel Maclane, but we were happy to still be within whispering distance, should we need to talk to each other during class.

With the three troublemakers separated, the

class went on without incident, and when the bell rang, Miss Friedman asked Dylan to stay behind while the rest of us filed out to find our lockers before the next class. Max's locker was down a different hallway, but mine was just a few steps away from our homeroom so I was fiddling with the combination lock when the door opened and Dylan and Miss Friedman came out, I managed to catch the tail end of their conversation as Miss Friedman appeared to be warning him that if he didn't behave this year, there were going to be serious consequences, Dylan hung his head and the look of fear in his eyes made him look apologetic but also vulnerable, breaking down his "tough-guy" facade. When Miss Friedman finally went back into the class and shut the door, Dylan stared through the door and mumbled under his breath *Bitch,* and gave her the finger through the window. I couldn't help but to look over at him upon hearing it, when our gazes met, and Dylan made his way over to me looking angry.

I looked away quickly and tried to pretend I was really focused on my lock, but Dylan saw right through my ruse and he nudged me on the shoulder when he got close enough.

What are you looking at? See something interesting? He asked in a confrontational tone.

69

No, I'm sorry, I didn't mean to listen, it was an accident. I responded, avoiding eye contact for fear of him seeing it as a challenge.

Oh, it was an accident?   He said sarcastically... *Well I guess it's all good then.*

I could sense his sarcasm, but a part of me was hopeful that he'd let it slide, so I looked up at him slightly, hoping I could read some form of mercy on his face, but unfortunately, anger was still the predominant emotion on display.

In your dreams, loser... Then he pushed me up against the lockers and got his face really close to mine, I could smell his breath as he spoke quietly... *If I get in trouble because you told some-one I called Miss Friedman a bitch, I'll make sure it's the last thing you do.*

I had no intention of aggravating the situation any further, so I nodded my head and the genuine fear in my eyes must have been convincing because Dylan let go of me, and with a final domin-ant stare, he turned and walked away, leaving me with the sinking feeling in the pit of my stomach that I'd made an enemy and that he had a lot of power in this school, so I was going to regret it very soon.

My next class was English and I didn't recognize anyone in the room, so I sat quietly and reflected on how unfortunate I had been to have accidentally pissed off Dylan and I worried about how this situation was going to play out. I concluded that the best course of action was to make myself invisible for a little while and avoid any contact with Dylan and his gang, at least until I had a few more friends to back me up if something were to go down.

Lunch came and I ran into Maggie near my locker, so we decided to find a quiet place to eat together where I could tell her what happened and hopefully get her support. We sat down in the grass near the soccer field and she told me that Dylan was in her second class with Tristan and that she thought he was a real jerk. She also told me that Max was in the same class and that she saw the three of them leave together for lunch and that she was worried that Tristan and Max would both become jerks too if they hung out with him, and just in that moment, a small crowd of boys came out of the building and started to make their way towards us.

As they approached, I recognized Dylan and his crew, trailed closely by Tristan and Max, both looking uncomfortable, they were each trying to look anywhere but at us and it appeared like they were trying to lag intentionally.

Maggie and I were pretty exposed and there was no doubt that they were headed right for us, looking around, I saw a few other students take notice of the situation and turn to get a better view of the show that was about to start. I looked over at Maggie and for some reason a look of determination was anchored to her face, but I was unfortunately not as confident about the outcome of the ensuing confrontation. My palms began to sweat and I could feel my heart racing in my chest as they approached.

When they got within earshot, Dylan yelled out:

Hey, Loser, I thought I told you to keep your mouth shut.

I was confused as to what he meant and it must have shown on my face, because when he got closer, he began to elaborate

I have to go to Principal Newridge's office after school today, this better not be about what you heard me call Miss Friedman...

I hadn't told on him but somehow I wasn't confident that he would see my innocence in all of this.

I swear, I didn't snitch Dylan. I responded, my voice shaking quite violently

Suddenly, Maggie got up and stood between Dylan and me, and despite the noticeable size difference between them, Maggie did her best to stare him down as she crossed her arms and gave him an angry look

Listen Dylan, he says he didn't do it, why don't you leave him alone and pick on somebody your own size.

Looking somewhat surprised and somewhat amused by Maggie's confidence, Dylan took a slight step back into his pack of goons and laughed at her attempt at defending me.

Oh, so Loser's got a girlfriend to fight his battles for him... He turned his head slightly to speak over his shoulder, but he didn't break eye contact with me... *That's surprising,* cause I was sure he was a FAG.

He emphasized the last word loudly and his friends all broke out in laughter, he waited a moment for them to quiet down a bit before he continued:

Come on guys, let's leave fag-boy and his girlfriend to finish their date, there will be plenty of time for a beating later if it turns out ratted on me.

Still chuckling, the pack turned and began to walk back towards the school, leaving Maggie fuming and me completely terrified of what might happen if they decided I was their target for the year.

As he walked by, Dylan put an arm on each of Max and Tristans shoulders, guiding them to follow the group, but before they had completely turned around, I caught a glimpse of Max's face and it was clear that he was avoiding eye contact, leaving me to believe that he wanted nothing to do with me or my current situation, causing a feeling of abandonment to form in the pit of my stomach.

Maggie waited until they were gone before she finally sat back down on the grass. She still looked really angry but her expression changed to a look of pity when she saw my face. My eyes had begun to well up now that they had left and their threats were ringing in my head. Most of all, my heart was really hurting because Max had chosen to be friends with Dylan instead of me.

That guy is a real jerk... She mumbled to herself,

then she paused slightly before turning her attention to me, she put her hand on my arm and tried to cover up the anger in her voice as she spoke *Don't worry, I'm sure he's in trouble for some other dumb thing he did.*

Fortunately, Dylan wasn't in any of my afternoon classes, but when I got to my last class, I saw Max sitting with Tristan and Big-Rig, so I took an empty seat near the door, hoping they wouldn't notice me. The teacher didn't bother with assigned seats, so we got to stay separated, but for the whole duration of the class, I had to fight the urge to look over at Max to confirm whether or not he had seen me. I wanted to find out why he was with them, but I didn't want to risk attracting Big-Rig's attention, because it would surely cause me trouble when the bell rang.

When school finally ended, I left quickly, and ran down to the front door of the school, hoping my mom would be there and we could make a quick getaway before Dylan or any of his goons could catch up to me. Fortunately, when I got to the designated pick-up spot, My mom's car was sitting at the front of the row and I wasted no time getting in and sinking down in my seat to avoid being seen as we pulled out of the parking lot.

How was your day sweetheart? My mom asked in a pleasant tone, totally unaware of the turmoil that was going on in my head.

I wasn't sure what to say, I didn't really have the energy to explain what had happened, that I'd made enemies with the bad-boys of the school, that they were threatening to beat me up at any given moment, that the only person who was my friend at the start of the day, had turned his back on me and was now a part of the guys who were tormenting me. There was no way to explain all of that and I certainly didn't want her to get freaked out and call the school, then they would definitely call me a rat. I said the only thing I could think of that wouldn't give her any information that I didn't want her to have:

It was fine.

I tried to sound convincing, I really didn't want any followup questions, because I knew I wasn't a very good liar and my mom would have me talking in no time.

A look of scepticism came across her face, but I must have been just convincing enough, because she decided to drop it, she could tell that I didn't really want to talk about something, but I don't think she suspected that anything was necessarily wrong. Instead, she began to talk about her own day and I pretended to listen, while my thought started to trail away to the events that went down earlier in the day.

I kept picturing Max's face while Dylan was threatening me at lunchtime, why wasn't he helping me? I thought about our sleepover and how much fun we had, and my heart began to sink as I pictured our fragile friendship falling apart. I had been so happy to have a friend who was so nice, and his family was so welcoming, and now without warning, he had turned stone cold and shut me out. I felt rejected and the pain was growing. Over the images in my head, I kept hearing Dylan's voice calling me a fag over and over again, and all his friends laughing. I'd heard people use that word before but I wasn't really sure what it meant, though based on the reaction it got, I was pretty certain it was meant as an insult.

By the time we arrived at our house, I was holding back tears, I grabbed my backpack and ran straight to my room, using homework as an excuse for my speedy exit, I closed my door and jumped on my bed to cry into my pillow, so that my mom wouldn't hear me and come asking what was wrong.

The second day
of school

◆ ◆ ◆

I must have fallen asleep while crying because the next thing I knew, I was waking up to the smell of bacon filling the walls of my room and the unmistakeable sizzle and pop, confirming that there was some cooking nearby. Usually, on a school day, My mom and I sat in silence and ate cereal for breakfast, but she must have thought I needed a special breakfast this morning because when I walked into the kitchen, I noticed that she had cooked a full array of food, including scrambled eggs, bacon, freshly pressed orange juice and what appeared to be hash brown coming out of the oven. When she noticed me, she turned around and gave me a concerned but sincere smile and asked how I was feeling in a genuine tone. Not wanting to let on that I was pretty bummed out, I mustered up the energy to lie to her again and responded

I'm fine mom... and then I tried to distract her by

changing the subject... *What's with the big break-fast?*

My mom thankfully decided to ignore my obvious fib and responded to my question instead

Oh, this?... She said looking over at the table full of food... *It's nothing, I just woke up early and felt like eating a big breakfast today, doesn't that sound good to you?*

I had to admit that it did.

We sat together at the table and she served me my share, I thanked her out loud for the breakfast and in my head for not pressing the issue of my obvious sadness. She talked to me about all the new friends she was making at her job and how they had even invited her out on Friday night. She had said that last part with an upward infliction, almost like she was asking me a question. I found out why almost immediately when she followed up with

So I was thinking that you could go sleep at your friend Max's house, that way I won't have to worry about you while I'm out with my friends. Does that sound like fun?

Something on my face must have changed because a frown came over her and she continued with more concern in her voice

What's wrong honey? I thought you'd be happy to spend the night at Max's place? Did something happen with you guys?

She was getting dangerously close to the truth, and I knew I had to throw her off the scent, so I faked enthusiasm in my response, hoping to buy myself some time.

No, nothing, sorry, I was thinking about a test I have today... Yeah, going to Max's sounds great, but are you sure his mom won't mind?

I was really hoping Max's mom would mind.

She seemed sceptical at my answer, maybe a test on the second day wasn't believable, but thankfully she chose to answer my question instead of asking one herself.

Not at all honey, I spoke with her last night after you went to bed, she said she'd be glad to have you over, it sounded like you and Max had so much fun together last time.

Damn, I guess I'd have to find another way out of this, fortunately Friday was still a few days away, so I was sure I could come up with something by then, but for now I'd have to fake enthusiasm, so that whatever excuse I came up with would be believable.

Great... Looking at the clock on the stove... *But I gotta go mom, I'm gonna be late for* school.

She double checked my assessment of the time and jumped when she saw that I was right. She quickly began to collect the dishes to deliver to the sink and told me to get ready for school, and that she'd meet me in the car in five minutes.

I ran to my room to get dressed and gather my school books, all the while kicking myself for not coming up with an excuse to get out of going to Max's place... Maybe Maggie would have some advice for me when I got to school.

When I got to the school yard, I looked all around to see if I could spot Maggie, but the first bell rang before I saw her, so I put my search on hold until lunchtime, because even if I found her at this point, I wouldn't have had the time to explain everything without being late for class.

I made my way quietly down the hall towards my homeroom with Miss Friedman, hoping not to encounter any of Dylan's goons until I was safely in the class, but unfortunately, when I turned the corner into the hall where my classroom and locker were, I saw Dylan, Big-Rig, Scar and Max standing by the door, presumably waiting for me

A. DIEL

to walk by so they could torture me some more. Having no alternative, other than skipping class to be able to avoid this interaction, I

sucked up all of my courage and walked in the direction of the likely onslaught.

Dylan would have had his meeting with Principal Newridge the night before and I was about to find out if they still thought I was a rat, worthy of sentencing to death.

Big-Rig was the first to spot me coming down the hall and I saw a chain of nudges and pointing making their way through the small group, and with every step that I took in their direction, My fears grew larger and larger about what might happen to me when I finally got within arms reach of them.

The three of them stared me down as I got closer, but Max stood off to the side, his presence showing solidarity, but his energy appeared to be protesting the stare down, in fact, he was looking at his feet, seeming to want to be anywhere but there.

I kept expecting Dylan to speak when I got close enough, the confrontation seemed inevitable, but his meeting with Newridge must have been about something else, because I walked all the way to the door, passed within inches of the group on my way to the classroom, and none of them intercepted me, they just continued to stare me down as if to remind me that I may not have been culpable of the crime I'd been accused of this time, but they were still keeping a close eye on me, and would not let me get away with anything.

As I took my seat, a sigh of relief escaped my mouth, I felt like I'd been pardoned from death-row. I knew in my heart that Dylan would not leave me alone, but I was just glad that this incident was over.

With the worry about my status as a rat leaving my mind, it left room for anger to take its place. Where there had been sadness the night before, regarding Max's betrayal of our friendship, I was now incredulous at how he could do this to me. I watched him follow the other three into the classroom once they'd been satisfied with their non-verbal warning towards me, and I couldn't help but feel rage growing inside me. Max was a traitor, he was a low-life who had chosen those idiots over me, and worst of all, he knew some of my secrets and it was only a matter of time before the whole school found out I was nothing but a cry-baby.

He sat down on the other side of our human buffer, the poor and unwilling participant Nathan Maclane, who had the misfortune of being born into a family who's name had placed him directly in the no -man's land of our battlefield, and attempted to get my attention with his eyes, but I held strong and gave him the coldest shoulder I could muster. I had no interest in speaking with someone who would turn their back on a friend in their time of need.

Throughout the lesson, I could feel his eyes on me, sensing that he wanted me to look over at him, presumably to reconnect after yesterday's betrayal, but I knew that if I relented and looked into his eyes, the memory of our time together as friends would make it very hard for me to uphold my anger, so I continued to ignore his attempts to get my attention.

When class let out, I quickly made my way to my locker to change my books in the hopes that I could be done before Max had a chance to catch up to me. I looked over and saw him standing with the other boys, clearly waiting for them to leave so he could come talk to me, but he didn't want to risk being seen fraternizing with me, so he had to wait until the coast was clear. Before he had a chance to break free from the huddle, I finished my book swap and turned away from the group, walking in the opposite direction of my next class; taking the long way around seemed like less of a hassle than walking past the cluster of bullies and having to face Max and the horrible feeling that was brewing inside me when I thought about him.

I managed to evade them for the whole morning and when lunch came, I went out to the field where Maggie and I had had sat the day before, in hopes of running into her and filling her in on the latest developments regarding my unspoken acquittal from earlier that morning and the upcoming weekend with Max.

Fortunately, when I walked outside, I saw her sitting in the field by herself, and when she spotted me, she perked up and waved me over.

Freddy, I've been looking for you, how did everything go with Dylan this morning?

I explained to her that it appeared that I was clear of any immediate danger for now, but that the Max's situation was really upsetting me, and that now, I'd have to spend the night at his house if I didn't come up with a way out of it.

She breathed in deeply before speaking, like she was about to walk out onto thin ice and holding her breath might make her lighter.

I don't know Freddy... Tristan and Max didn't really look like they wanted to be there yesterday, and even though you know how I feel about Tristan, I still think you should give them a chance to explain themselves.

Her response caught me off guard, and I couldn't, for the life of me, figure out why she was defending them.

What do you mean Maggie? They're clearly jerks, and I don't want anything to do with them. I retorted, stunned

It's just that... She paused for a moment, seeming to be unsure about whether or not to tell me the next part... *Max called me last night, and we talked for a long time, and he told me that he was really mad at himself about the whole thing, and...* Again she paused, trying to think of the best way to explain the rest... *I just think you should give him a chance to explain himself...*

Max was mad at himself? I hadn't really given much thought as to what he might be feeling; so far, I had spent most of my energy on how this affected me and why he would do this to me. Slowly my anger began to subside at the thought that he might have a valid excuse.

I don't know Maggie, what could he possibly say that would make what he did okay?

I was digging for more information.

Just trust me Freddy, you should hear what he has to say.

She wouldn't give me any more information, but her tone was sincere and it cast enough doubt in the situation for me to consider letting him have his day in court with me.

Just in that moment, the door to the school opened up and a slump-shouldered low-headed Max walked out, scouring the schoolyard for any signs of danger as he made his way towards us. He kept looking over his shoulder as he approached and when he finally reached us, he stopped and looked me in the eyes before opening his mouth to speak in a muted tone

Freddy, can I talk to you?

He sounded nervous, like he was fully expecting me to deny his request.

I looked over at Maggie, wanting her to assure me one more time that this was a good idea, and with a simple head nod, she compelled me to accept.

Fine... I said, trying to sound irritated... *Say what*

you have to say.

He looked over his shoulder again before continuing

Not here though, can we go somewhere more private? He pleaded, sounding desperate

No way... I shot back... *Whatever you have to say, you can say it right here, in front of Maggie.*

He looked defeated, letting out a pitiful sigh, his voice began to shake

Please Freddy, I promise I'll explain everything, just not here, it's important... He was practically begging at this point.

I looked over at Maggie, expecting her to share in my disbelief that he would try to manipulate the situation, but instead she gave me a slightly scornful look, like I was being unreasonable, and then she nodded her head sideways, as if to say *"Go with him you idiot"*.

So I got up, convincing myself that if Maggie told me to do it, I could always blame her if it didn't go well. I followed Max to the edge of the school-yard, where a batch of trees gave a little bit of shelter from the prying eyes of our peers, and without exchanging a single word, he led me further into the small forest until he felt like we were sufficiently far away, where he stopped dead in his tracks and turned around to finally face me. He opened his mouth, as if to speak, but nothing came out, like the words he was planning to use had mysteriously disappeared from his vocabulary at that exact moment.

What? I asked, the anger in my voice was pretty clear, I was getting tired of being strung along and I just wanted this to be over.

He broke the eye contact and dropped his head to stare at his feet, His shoulders came up and his head sank further into them, through a shaky and quiet voice I just barely heard him utter

I'm sorry.

I expected him to open with that, but I hadn't anticipated how it would make me feel, he had never appeared so submissive to me before, his pain was palpable as he stood there, clearly remorseful, and his sincerity nearly broke my heart. I felt so bad that I was the one making him feel this way. I didn't know how to respond, and when the silence began to grow a little long for his liking, he looked up to read my face, perhaps hoping that I would be receptive to his apology, and that's when I noticed the tear running down his cheek, which broke down the last morsel of anger that I had inside me. I leaned forward and put my arms around him, trying to hug away the pain this was causing him, effectively reversing the role from the first day that we met, where he comforted me. But it didn't feel like it was enough, so I hugged harder, and I felt his body grow limp, like the sadness that was encasing his heart had just suddenly left him and now I was able to feel him more closely. He put his face into my shoulder and I felt it getting wetter as he sobbed, so I moved a hand up to the back of his head, combing my fingers through his hair, hoping he would understand that I thought it was okay for him to cry. He just kept saying *I'm sorry, I'm sorry...* but the words were hard to understand because he was sobbing and speaking them into my shoulder.

We stood like that for a moment, feeling like more than just our bodies were touching, and when he finally lifted his head, wiping the tears from his face with the sleeve of his shirt, he sniffled a bit as he collected himself, and spoke in a substantially clearer tone.

I'm so sorry about yesterday Freddy... He paused for a moment and saw that I was giving him an opening to explain himself... *I didn't want to be a part of it at all, but when Tristan and me were talking after math class yesterday, Dylan and the other guys showed up to talk to Tristan and he introduced us. They were talking for a while and then they started talking about you and they were saying how you were a snitch and that they should beat you up. I should have said something, but I was scared of getting beat up too. I was about to come warn you, but Dylan put his arm on my shoulder and before I knew it, he was leading me out to the field where we saw you, and well... you know the rest.*

His voice had changed a bit throughout his explanation, switching between speaking really fast so I wouldn't have a chance to interject and speaking really quietly because he clearly felt so bad.

It kind of made sense to me, I wasn't exactly pleased with the outcome, but I understood that he didn't want to get beaten up. It wasn't either of our faults that those guys were picking on me, but I could see why being my friend could be disastrous for his fragile reputation right now.

So then what? We can't be friends anymore? I asked, a little hurt by the realization

Umm.... He looked uncomfortable with the answer he had to give.... *It's not that, I still want to be your friend, but... It's just that I'm not sure it's a good idea to be friends at school... if that's okay with you?*

I didn't have much choice, the alternative was to lose him as a friend altogether. I wanted things to be different, but unfortunately this was my best option. I sighed.

I guess... My dissatisfaction was pretty obvious.

Are you sure? He asked, and then continued with... *We can still be friends outside of school, and you can still come over to my house and read my comic books and go swimming.* He sounded excited at the prospect of getting the best of both worlds.

This was not ideal, and I was a little hurt at the proposal, but I knew I had no other options, so I put a fake smile on and nodded my head. Immediately I saw relief in his eyes, and the smile he returned was worth the slight pain that our new arrangement was causing me. In his excitement, he jumped forward and hugged me, this time, he was the one squeezing while I let my arms dangle limply, it felt good but part of me felt like I would be lying if I hugged back.

When we got back to the field where Maggie was still sitting, Max shot me a final look of satisfaction and broke off to head back into the building, I finished my walk back to Maggie alone, and when I arrived, she broke my ponderous focus with a question

So? What happened? She looked proud, like she already knew the answer to her question.

I had a lot of thoughts and feelings flying through my head, I was still reeling from my anger, which had mostly been replaced with joy, since Max and I had worked things out a bit, but now I also felt a bit of shame, like I was his secret friend, and I had to be willing to hide my true feelings for him, depending on the circumstances. It felt wrong somehow, but I wasn't sure how to express that to Maggie.

You were right. Was all I said, Unable to find words to explain the rest of my thought, and assured that this would be enough for her to drop it.

I knew it! She exclaimed... *See don't you feel better now?*

But I didn't, this was just a new, different bad feeling.

Yeah, I do... I lied.

The rest of the week went on without any major incidents, whenever I saw Max in the halls, he checked to make sure no one was watching before smiling at me and saying hi. Each time,

I smiled back but the feeling of shame grew stronger. I continued to stay clear of Dylan and his goons whenever possible, and the tension seemed to ease slightly when we were in class together.

Maggie and I continued to eat lunch together every day in the field, and as the week wore on, she talked more and more about Max until I began to get the impression that she might have feelings for him that were more than just friend-like. Finally, on the Friday, I decided to ask her straight up, my curiosity was too strong to ignore, and I just couldn't be left wondering any more.

Hey, so... do you like Max?

She froze like a statue when I asked this and her cheeks began to turn red.

Of course I like Max, he's a good friend... She tried to play it off like she was answering the question I had asked, but we both knew that's not what I had meant.

No, I mean, do you LIKE Max? Like, "like him" like him?

Now her face was fully scarlet, she began to fiddle with the laces on her shoes.

I don't know... I mean... She looked up at me... *Do you think he likes me?*

I hadn't thought about it, the idea of them liking each other had never crossed my mind and when I tried to picture it, I felt some strange discomfort in the pit of my stomach, but I wasn't sure why.

Hey! She interrupted my thoughts, *You're going to sleep over at his house tonight, right? Do you think you can find out?*

I had no desire to, but I couldn't possibly tell her that, so I lied

Sure... I guess

Awesome! You're the best... She said, sounding more chipper than I'd ever heard her sound. With that, she jumped at me and put her arms around my neck, clearly thankful for the favour that I hadn't performed yet.

I didn't know how to react so I patted her lightly on the back until she released me.

We finished our lunch relatively quietly and then the bell rang, announcing that it was time for us to go back to class, but as I was walking away, she yelled out

Hey Freddy... And waited for me to turn around before continuing... *Don't forget...* Not needing to go into anymore detail about what I was meant to remember.

I nodded my head, but on the inside, I wished I had never asked her if she liked him.

Max's house
(part 2)

◆ ◆ ◆

My mom Picked me up at the end of the day, and in the backseat I could see my overnight bag, which I didn't remember packing, so it probably didn't have the right clothes in it. I was grateful for the gesture, so I decided not to broach the subject.

She announced to me that since it was a little early to be going to Max's place right now, she was going to take me out for ice cream first, and that when we were done, she would drive me to my sleepover, which I thought was a pretty good idea, seeing as how ice cream always made me happy.

Unfortunately, I wasn't able to fully enjoy my cold treat, because I was still unsure about how this sleep-over would go, Max had been avoiding me in public all week and he'd been really nice to me when no one else was around, I wasn't sure if

I was going to be able to truly enjoy his company knowing that it had to come to an end when we got back to school on Monday.

I really liked Max, but I wasn't sure if I wanted to be a secret part-time friend, and it was getting harder and harder for me to imagine a scenario where we could really have fun this weekend.

My mom clearly sensed that something was wrong, but she'd been getting used to my side-stepping whenever she asked me how I was doing, so instead, she tried to distract me by goofing around and trying to make me laugh. When she saw that it wasn't working, she finally decided to confront the elephant in the room and she showed me the more serious side of her that I hadn't seen since my dad died.

You know Freddy, I've been noticing that something is bothering you, and I know I'm not the one you want to talk to about it, cause I'm your mom and "that would be lame"... She said that last part in a dopey voice, pausing to see if I was amused before getting serious again... *But I want you to know that if there's ever anything you need to talk about, you can talk to me about it.*

I was a little surprised at this, she was being so genuine, we didn't really talk much like this anymore, but all of a sudden, I felt like she was on my team, like maybe when I understood what I was feeling, it would be okay to tell her about it. I guess I must have been staring at her a little blank-faced, because she followed up with.

You got that little-man?

"Little-man" was what my dad used to call me, she was trying it out for the first time and I didn't hate it, it felt kind of nice to hear it again, even though it wasn't from him. The feeling it gave me caused me to smile a little, so I acknowledged her statement

Thanks mom, I got it.

Promise? She asked, to confirm our agreement

Promise. I responded in acknowledgement.

In that moment, I truly felt like I would talk to her as soon as I could make sense of this whole thing.

When we got to Max's house, his dad and brother were outside, pouring themselves over the engine compartment of a pretty beat up older car that more closely resembled the one we were arriving in than any car that belonged in that driveway. I got out and the both of them greeted me with their patented family smile, and when I got closer, Tyler called me over, beaming with pride

Hey Freddy, check it out... He said, waving his hand in the direction of the car... *We just picked her up, She needs a bit of work before she's legal for the road but by this time next week, she'll be purring like a kitten and tearing up the roads!*

...At or below the legal speed limit... Interrupted his father, talking to his son, but looking at my mother with a slight eye-roll, clearly repeating something he'd already said a thousand times

Right... Tyler corrected himself ... *"At or below the legal speed limit"...* He continued, mimicking his father's scornful tone.

We all laughed at Tyler's imitation, Then his dad told me that Max was up in his room.

Thanks mister Longview... I said, as I gave my mom a covert "goodbye" head nod and turned to walk into the house

Hey! I heard his voice calling me back, so I turned around... *I thought I told you to call me Scott...* He said, half-jokingly

I laughed a little at myself for forgetting... *You're right, I'm sorry, Thank you SCOTT...* I emphasized his name, to indicate that I would try to remember next time.

I walked into the air conditioned house and made my way to the stairs leading up to Max's room, I still wasn't sure how it would feel to be with him outside of school, part of me was worried that his friendship wouldn't feel genuine and that I'd have a hard time getting over that, but as soon as I walked into his room and he saw me, he jumped off the bed and ran up to me to give me a hug, which was powerful enough to alleviate at least some of my fear.

I set my bag down and he just sat back on his bed and watched me with a huge grin on his face, like he was surprised that I was even here, in the flesh, but then his smile faded and he kind of got a bit serious.

Freddy, I'm so happy you're here, but I can't help but think about how much I hate the way it has to be at school.

Wow, I couldn't believe that he'd just jumped right into that subject, and that we shared that opinion, I thought he was happy about our arrangement, so it surprised me to find out that this was hard on him too, and I'm sure it must have come through in my voice as I answered him

Yeah... Me too...

It's just that... He paused for a moment... *It tears me up inside that I have to be mean to you... like ever... because I don't want anything bad to happen to you, but I don't know what to do to stop it...* He said the last part to himself, like he was just thinking out loud.

This revelation of his true feelings was really making me feel closer to him, like our friendship was really holding strong beneath all of the other stuff that had gone on in the week. It was enough for me and I didn't want him to be sad anymore, so I tried to change the subject

I appreciate that Max... He looked up at me... *I really do, but let's not worry about that now, we're not there right now, we're here, so let's just be friends and we'll deal with that other stuff later...* I could tell that he was starting to come out of his slump, so I finished off with... *Plus, it's still way too hot out, and you promised me I could swim in your pool...*

With that, the seriousness completely left his face and his trademark smile beamed back at me, both of us feeling that this issue had been resolved and that we could now just go on being ourselves.

You're right man, those trunks I lent you are still

in the changing shack, let's go!

His excitement was contagious, he leapt off of his bed and bolted out the door, with me just trying to keep up behind him, as we ran past his mom in the kitchen, and she tried to greet me, he yelled out

NO TIME MOM, WE'RE GOING SWIMMING!

She seemed shocked but slightly amused, but I still made it a point to be as polite as possible in passing
Sorry Misses Longview, it's very nice to see you, but Max is in a rush!

She acknowledged my attempt at staying behind, but then nodded in the direction of the backdoor, as if to say "what are you waiting for?", so I continued out to the backyard.

When I got into the change room, Max was just tying the string on his swimsuit and he ran out the door as soon as he was done, leaving me with

Don't take too long, I'll be waiting on the roof!

It was impossible to ignore his enthusiasm at the moment, so I hurried to put on the swimsuit that had been left in the spare cubby from the last time I was here, and as I walked out onto the pool deck and made my way around to the stairs leading up to the roof, I heard Tyler's voice as he was coming out of the house

Hey! Why didn't you guys tell me you were going swimming?

From behind me, atop his rock, I heard Max respond

Sorry Tyler, it was a snap decision, do you want us to wait for you before we jump?

No way man, get after it, I'll be out in a minute... Tyler responded, almost scoffing at the idea of us waiting for him.

He made his way into the change room, just as I was reaching the top of the stairs and Max came into view on the edge of the rock, he was looking back at me with his hand extended out, he must have known that I would need encouragement to jump off again, it had been a week since the last time and my fear was creeping back in.

He took me by the hand and pulled me to the edge, then I looked at him for reassurance, and he must have understood completely, because he responded with

Don't worry, I won't let anything bad happen to you here.

I nodded my head and he counted us down...3... 2...1... and for the first time, the two of us jumped at the same time, neither of us pulling the other, we were taking the leap together and it felt exhilarating.

Not long after, Tyler came out of the changing area and began to run around the pool over to the rock we had just jumped from, as he ran, Max pulled me towards the shallow end, away from the landing zone and said

Come this way, and watch this... As he nodded his head in Tyler's direction, who had now disappeared from our sight up the stairs.

Without warning, a loud yell came from above us, and a running Tyler came into view. He placed his final step on the very edge of the rock and pushed off, swinging his free leg forward, making him do a backflip in the air, while falling forward. It seemed like he was flying in slow motion, I'd never seen anything like it. His feet came around underneath him and he landed in the water with almost no splash, It was almost like the professional divers in the olympics. My eyes and mouth must have been wide open with amazement because I looked over at Max and he said

I know, right? He's awesome!

We both laughed at that, and while we were distracted, Tyler swam under the surface towards us and all of a sudden, a hand was grabbing my ankle and pulling me underwater. When I opened my eyes, I saw that max had suffered the same fate and that Tyler was the one holding us down and looking devilishly proud of himself.

He released us and when the three of us surfaced, Max immediately seemed to flex his entire body in anticipation, like he knew what was coming next, but I had no clue what was about to happen so I watched in awe as Tyler grabbed Max below the ribs and easily picked him up out of the water, before launching him backwards into the deep end. Max screamed and laughed the whole way into the water and Tyler couldn't help but giggle at his brother's reaction. I couldn't believe how strong Tyler was, but I was about to get a first hand taste of it because as soon as Max was fully submerged from his fall, Tyler turned his attention towards me and I froze in place as he approached. Almost identically to the way he had just thrown his brother, Tyler grabbed me and hoisted me out of the water, but since I was smaller, he managed to throw me substantially farther than Max. Flying backwards, I got almost the same feeling in my stomach as when we jumped off the rock and it felt like I was flying forever.

Max and Tyler were both looking at me with anticipation in their eyes when I wiped the water from my face and was able to see again, I think they were worried that I would have disliked being thrown around, but I wanted to assure them that it had been fun, so I hollered out

Man! That was awesome!

The brothers both looked at each other and laughed, relieved that they hadn't overstepped
my comfort zone.

We continued to rough-house, with Tyler easily winning every battle, even when Max and I decided to team up to try to take him down. When we were sufficiently tired, Tyler suggested that we go inside to see if dinner was ready, so we all went to the change room to shower off the chlorine and get changed.

Walking inside, we were hit with a wonderful and familiar smell, and Max's mom poked her head out of the kitchen to announce that they had ordered pizza and that it had just arrived.

During the meal, Tyler told loud stories that made everyone laugh and I noticed Max watching his brother speak with admiration, making me envy the love that they shared for each other.

After dinner, we went up to Max's room to play video games and we got into our pyjamas to settle in on the floor where we had set up our sleeping area like the last time I was over.

While we were playing, a question kept coming back up in my mind and I couldn't hold it in any longer, because I'd been thinking about it all week.

Hey Max, do you remember when you guys came out on Monday while me and Maggie were eating?

Max's virtual car stopped moving on the track and he looked over at me, he seemed hesitant to answer, because he wasn't sure if I was going to bring up something unpleasant

...umm...yeah...

I tried to reassure him that I wasn't mad or anything

No, no, it's nothing bad... it's just that... I paused slightly, because I didn't want to seem stupid for asking this, but he was literally the only person that I could trust with this question... *well, remember, Dylan called me a fag, right?* I paused again, his face was telling me to go on

...um, yeah, I remember...

Well... I don't know... what does that mean... is it bad?

Max looked a little uncomfortable, which was a bit of a relief, because I was worried that he'd think I was an idiot for not knowing something.

To be honest, I didn't know either... he started... *So I asked Tyler, and he said that it's like...* he paused shifting slightly... *A bad word for when...* he paused again, like he wished he didn't have to say the next part... *a guy likes another guy.* His face had turned bright red during the course of his explanation, but I couldn't figure out what had made him so uncomfortable.

Well that doesn't sound so bad, I like other guys... I said, not fully understanding why that would cause an issue, I liked Max and he was a guy...

A look of defeat came over him, like he was going to have to elaborate, but he really didn't want to go into any more detail.

No, I mean like when a guy "likes" another guy... You

know, like "likes him" likes him... He winced a little as he watched my face while explained himself, like he knew that he was describing something new to me and he was expecting my actual brain to explode in front of his eyes.

The reality of what he was describing began to set in, I didn't know that was possible. I had always thought that guys liked girls and that girls liked guys, the idea that guys could like other guys wasn't something that had ever crossed my mind. I tried to wrap my head around what that would mean for them and slowly, I began to wonder if I liked other guys like that. I tried to think of any girls that I thought were really special to me and other than the friendship with Maggie, I couldn't come up with anything, and then I started to think about my feelings for Max and a lot of questions were suddenly being answered, and I started to realize that maybe I did like Max more than I thought.

My face began to feel warm, I knew it was turning red with embarrassment, and there was nothing I could do to stop it from happening.

Did that make me a fag?

It did not sound like something that I wanted to be... the way Dylan made that word come out of his mouth, and the way his friends laughed when he said it, that didn't sound like a word I ever wanted to be called again. Shame started to set in because it was becoming clear to me that I might be a fag, but that wasn't something that other people would be cool with.

It dawned on me that that Max had been watching my face as I processed the information, and that he would be getting suspicious of what might be going on in my head, and the last thing I wanted was for Max to think I was a fag, because then he might never want to be friends with me again. I thought I'd better say something to change the subject, but all I could hear in my thoughts was Dylan calling me a fag, and me starting to believe it.

Max must have known that I wanted to say something because he looked at me in anticipation, but nothing was coming out, and the fact that I had nothing to say was making it pretty obvious to me that I was basically admitting to being a fag.

The longer this wore on the less I knew what to say, I felt the moment for defending myself was slowly melting away, all I had to say was "*I'm not a fag*", but I couldn't seem to formulate that sentence, and my resolve to speak was being replaced by shame for my new realization.

I put my head down because Max surely knew what was happening by now and I couldn't possibly face him, he was probably disgusted with me for being a fag and was trying to come up with a way to get me to leave.

A single tear rolled down my face, but I held back a sob as hard as I could because in my mind, crying about it was leaving no doubt whatsoever, but unfortunately, my emotions got the better of me and I put my face into my hands to hide it and my tears really began to flow as I cried softly.

It felt like an eternity before I felt a familiar hand on my shoulder, it was the hand that had comforted me in this very room the last time I was here. It was a hand that was trying to tell me that it didn't matter, that it was alright to cry. I gained a bit of strength from his hand, because there was no doubt in my mind that he understood what was happening and that it was still trying to make me feel better.

I looked up slightly to see if Max's face was as accepting as his hand and when I saw him, he had tears running down his face as well.

I was confused, why would Max be crying? I was crying because I'd just found out I was a fag and it wasn't a very good thing to be, but he had no reason to be crying... unless...

His hand pulled me forward slightly and he leaned his head towards mine. When our faces were almost touching, my eyes darted back and forth between is lips and his eyes, trying to find meaning in his actions. My heart was racing and it felt like it was trying to escape my chest with every beat. I was looking for any trace of a smile that would indicate that he might be making a cruel joke or something, but while I was contemplating whether or not he was being genuine, he closed the gap between us and our lips met for the first time.

His skin was soft and he was breathing heavily through his nose, as if he was trying to inhale me, his eyes were closed and he was squeezing them shut with such intensity. I felt his smooth lips on my own and my stomach felt like it was doing backflips. I thought it would be impossible for my heart to beat any faster, but this kiss was making it feel like it was going to explode. This was a feeling that I could not have anticipated if someone had tried to describe it to me, it felt so right to be sharing this kiss with Max, like when two pieces of a puzzle fit together and make their odd shaped sides disappear into a beautiful picture.

In that moment, the door to Max's room burst open and Tyler's voice came in loudly

Hey, good night bo... He stopped dead in his tracks and his tone changed completely... *Oh... sorry...*

Max and I separated like a grenade had gone off between us, landing us as far away from each other as we could possibly get in a single motion. We both felt the shame creeping back in and began to stare at our hands intensely. Almost immediately, Max began to cry again, and hearing him sob made it impossible for me not to follow suit. I heard the door shut softly and Tyler's voice continued from inside the room.

Hey, hey, hey... don't cry, it's okay... He got closer to us and knelt down to our level, he placed a hand on each of our shoulders, causing us both to look up at him through watery eyes with hope, he reiterated... *It's okay!*

Max interrupted in protest with a shaky voice... *But this means we're fags, and everyone will hate us...*

Tyler tightened his grip on our shoulders and inhaled sharply, as if Max's words had hurt him, and he looked directly into his little brother eyes

First of all, fag is a terrible word and I don't want to hear you saying it, say gay instead. He sounded like he was scolding his Max for being mean to himself, but then he softened slightly, *Secondly, there's nothing wrong with being gay, it's just something that makes you different, not worse. And thirdly, but most important of all, "I" don't hate you...* He said that very seriously, leaving no room for alternate interpretation... *In fact, I love you, and if this is what makes you happy, then I'm happy for you...* He looked over at me... *BOTH of you...* He wanted to make sure that I felt included... *And I want you to know that nothing you can do or say will ever change that... You got it?*

Max looked at his brother, his hope restored that at least he was on our side.

You mean that? He spoke quietly, while wiping a tear from his cheek

Yeah, of course I mean that Kiddo... He looked back at me before continuing... *And if anyone gives you guys any problems, or calls you guys fags, you tell them that I'll be having a talk with them, and that's a promise.* He said "having a talk" but he had put up his fist, implying that the chat would be physical

Max looked up at Tyler once again, this time assured that everything was going to be okay, and with a sight of relief, he jumped at his neck and hugged him as hard as he could. Tyler wanted me to know that his promise was true for me as well, so with his free hand, he pulled me into max's hug and a feeling of security came over me as his strong arms held us in close and his promise echoed in our hearts.

When we separated from our three-way hug, Tyler took a moment to stare at each of us in the eyes and wipe the last tears from our cheeks. His eyes seemed to be cementing his point that he was serious about being on our team and I think he just wanted to make sure that that was clear.

Well, it's been a big day boys, I'm gonna go to bed, you guys should probably do the same.

We quietly nodded our heads in approval, and as he was leaving the room, he turned around one last time

Remember, I love you guys. Good night.

In unison, we responded

Good night Tyler.

When he finally shut the door, I let out a huge sigh of relief, Tyler was right, it had been a big day. Max and I looked at each other, but it was hard to find words to explain what we were feeling, so we just stared at each other quietly and smiled. There was a new feeling in my heart, one that felt like freedom, like my heart was an eagle, soaring above mountains and rivers, I felt so light. I had finally unearthed what had been bothering me for so long, and worked it out with Max. And now, we had told Tyler, and he was on our side, the world felt right to me for a moment.

I laid down in my sleeping bag and thought about the kiss Max and I had shared, I never knew my body could react to anything that way, like waves of electricity were shooting to every extremity of my being. A smile crept over my face, and as I was dosing off into sleep, I felt a hand interlace with my own, and I succumbed to sleep, feeling like I had been reconnected with my other half.

Coming clean

◆ ◆ ◆

When I woke up the next morning, our hands were still connected, and looking over, I saw that Max had the biggest grin on his face as he slept, reassuring me that the kiss we shared the night before was equally enjoyed by the both of us and that he hadn't started to regret it during the night.

Soon after, Max awoke and softly giggled when he noticed that we were still holding hands, before turning to me and wishing me a good morning.

While we were getting changed into our day clothes, Max turned and asked me a question which caught me off guard.

Hey, so, do you want to be here when I tell my parents I'm gay, or would you rather me wait until after you leave?

I was floored that he was thinking of telling his parents right away, we'd only just found out last night that we were both gay, and it seemed too soon to be telling anyone.

What do you mean? You're going to tell them right now? I asked, hoping that I'd misunderstood

Well yeah, I mean, as long as you're cool with it...

Doesn't this all seem... I don't know... too soon? This wasn't making any sense to me, wasn't being gay wrong? Wouldn't his parents be mad? What if they stopped loving him? What if they kicked him out? He'd have to come live at my place I suppose, but surely my mom couldn't afford to feed all three of us.

He could see the wheels turning in my head, he was starting to get used to witnessing my brain working a thousand miles per minute, so he placed a hand on my arm, as if to ground me, and spoke softly, in a tone he knew would calm me down a little.

Yeah, maybe, but I don't want to lie to my parents, that sounds awful, plus, I'm gay, that's me, so they should know that.

But what if it's just a phase? What if we're not really gay?

He paused for a moment, searching for the right words.

I always thought I might be gay I just didn't know there was a word for it. The first time we met, I got a strange feeling that I had never gotten before in the pit of my stomach. Spending time with you has always felt good, but it also felt like we were never quite close enough, like there was something missing. Then, last night, when we kissed, it felt like the rest of it was there, like it was the most right thing that could ever happen. There's no turning back now Freddy, that kiss made everything finally make sense to me...

There it was. He had summed up exactly what I had been trying to put into words. It did make sense, it filled in all the blank spaces and answered all of the questions I had.

...But if you're not ready to tell anyone, I understand, I can wait until you leave before I talk to them... He continued

I thought about it. He was right, it didn't seem right to lie. Plus, if we told his parents and it didn't go well, at least we had Tyler on our side... and I could always go home and not tell my mom, just pretend it didn't happen.

I guess it's alright. I responded sheepishly.

His patented smile made an appearance across his face, reassuring me slightly, and the rest of the work was done by his words:

Don't worry, my parents will be fine with it, it'll all be okay, I promise.

Walking down the stairs towards the kitchen, I could hear his Mother and Father having a conversation, but my heart was beating too loudly in my head to make out what they were saying. As we approached the doorway to the kitchen, I slowed right down, second guessing whether or not I really wanted to do this... there was still time to get out of it, no one would know but Tyler, and something told me that he would guard our secret pretty closely if we asked him to.

Max noticed that I wasn't keeping pace and turned around to see what was wrong. When he saw the hesitation in my face, he walked back to me and took my hand in his, staring into my eyes, trying to telepathically give me some of his confidence. The contact from his skin helped slightly, and he started walking again, gently dragging me by the hand, but not pulling like he did that first time in the pool. The way he walked without hesitation made me admire him even more, he didn't seem afraid at all, even though this was probably the scariest thing either of us had ever faced.

As we entered the kitchen, we saw his parents sitting across the island from each other, Max's dad was pointing to an article in the paper that he'd laid out on the counter and turned towards his wife so that she could read it. They both turned to wish us a good morning and saw that Max and I were holding hands. I was dividing my stare equally between their faces, to gauge their reaction, overcome with fear and shame, but out of the corner of my eye, I could see that Max was standing tall, with his chest out, like he was ready for battle, should it come, and in that moment, he squeezed my hand tightly, as if to say "I'll protect you if anything happens"

A small gasp escaped his mother's mouth. Needless to say, she was surprised.

His Father was the first to break the silence.

Good morning boys... He nodded his head in the direction of our hands... *What's going on here?*

He didn't sound angry, or even disappointed; in

fact, he sounded almost amused, like he already knew the answer to his question, and that it would make him happy, but that he was holding that happiness back until he heard it from his son.

I heard Max take a deep breath and release it, fortifying his courage.

Mom, Dad, I have something I want to say... He paused, his voice had quieted a bit at the end there, he was losing his nerve.

His mom chimed in *What is it sweetie? You know you can tell us anything.* Her voice was sweet and soft, like the voice one might use to get an unfamiliar dog to approach you so you can pet him. Unthreatening, just calm and comforting.

I took this as my cue to help, I looked over at Max and squeezed his hand tightly, returning all of the courage he'd loaned me before we walked in, then I nodded my head, as if to say "You can do it Max, I believe in you"

I guess this was all he needed. He took another deep breath, this one more stable, and let it out. Looking back to his parents, his eyes darted back and forth between them and then said the bravest thing I'd ever heard anyone say

...I'm gay.

Immediately the room felt quiet, almost too quiet, and Max's hand tightened its grip, I could feel his faltering confidence through my hand. His head dropped, and his eyes began to well up. I wanted to hold him tight, and make him feel better, I wanted to tell him that it was going to be okay, that they could forsake us both completely, and that it didn't matter, because we had each other, but in that moment, I got mad at them. How could they let their son cry? How could they watch his pain like this and do nothing?

I looked over at them with rage in my eyes, I was seeing red, but to my surprise, when I saw their faces, they were looking at each other, smiling through tears.

Both got up from their stools and walked over to Max and covered him with their conjoined bodies, forming a forcefield to protect him from evil with their love. The only piece of him that remained visible was his hand protruding from the huddle, still firmly gripped into my own, through which I could feel their love radiating and crawling up my arm.

Between sobs, I heard his mother whisper into his

ear

We know baby, it's okay, we're just happy you told us.

The hug continued and its intensity was magnetic, I was beginning to feel like a third wheel when Scott turned his attention towards me.

What about you Freddy, are you gay too?

It was so blunt, such a direct question, but he posed in in a way that made it seem like he already knew the answer, and that this was my opening to say it out loud safely.

My eyes got misty, and I tried to say the words "yeah, I am gay" but nothing came out, so I resolved to nod my head in the affirmative, Scott smiled from ear to ear and his free arm reached behind me and pulled me into their family hug. After some slight shifting, I found myself in the middle, My arms naturally making their way around Max, who was now warm from being in the centre of the huddle, and his body was limp, having torn down all of the thick walls he'd put up around his heart to protect his secret.

Never before had I felt so understood, I'd told these people all of the things I knew about myself, had held nothing back, and they had accepted me for all of it. It finally felt like it was okay to be me, the real me, without any secrets or shame, and it felt wonderful.

When the tears were all wiped clean and the hug ended, we all naturally gravitated to the kitchen island where we took our seats and Max's mom served us all breakfast. We sat in relative silence, exchanging meaningful looks between each other, expressing gratitude and acceptance. I was feeling drained, like I'd been holding a heavy rock over my head my entire life and now, finally, I'd been given permission to let it fall to the ground and walk away from it. I was relieved to be rid of it, but a part of me thought it might come back when I faced my mom... or the bullies at school...

What if Dylan found out? He'd have a field day with this... He was already prepared to harass me day and night before having anything to legitimately lord over my head, but now this? this was the mother of all mothers when it comes to bullying.

I must have changed expressions, because Scott took note of my face and immediately asked what was wrong.

I tried to explain what was going through my head, but the words were jumbled. Max's house felt safe, it was legitimately the only place in the world where I could be myself and be accepted, like a small island in the middle of shark infested waters, but the fear of facing the real world was consuming me, and it was impossible to express how terrifying the whole thing was. Scott let me try to speak, he sat quietly, attentively, and tried to make sense of the few words that came out clearly

Mom... Dylan... School...Dead.

I looked over at Max, and the reality of what I was saying started to set into his psyche too, his face changed dramatically when I said Dylan's name, like a dark cloud had just appeared above his head.

Scott sat back in his chair and took in the information that he was extrapolating from my babbling, and from the new expression on his youngest son's face, but then a look of delight came over his face as he appeared to have come to a conclusion. He jumped out of his chair and ran out of the room, only to return with an old dusty book in his hands and a smile on his face. He flipped quickly to a dog-eared page in the book and exclaimed

Ah! Here it is!

Max and I shared a quizzical look before turning

back to his dad with anticipation.

I knew this would come in handy one day... He said to himself, before turning his attention to us... *Bernard Baruch! Words to live by boys,* then he cleared his throat and spoke loudly like he was in a stage play " *Those who matter don't mind, and those who mind don't matter"!*

He closed the book with conviction, looking pleased with himself that he'd solved our problem once and for all, but our faces must have shown that we were still quite confused, because he took to explaining himself right away.

You see boys, what Baruch was saying is that anyone who's important in your life will understand, and they won't have any problems with you being gay, and anyone who does have a problem with it, isn't someone who should be important to you... why would you want to be friends with them anyway? Does that make sense?

The clarification had helped, as the words sank in, it became clear to me that Dylan and his goons didn't matter, that they might have an impact on my life right now, but that one day, I'd be moving on to bigger and better things, and they'd probably still be scraping their knuckles on the ground and picking fleas off of each other.

The image of Big-Rig and Scar as apes made me laugh a little, and Max gave me a half smile with an inquisitive look

I'll explain later... I whispered, in answer to his unasked question, it seemed to appease him.

Not long after breakfast, my mom arrived to pick me up, just as Tyler was emerging from his adolescent slumber. While we stood in the foyer, with my mom at the front door, and Max's entire family looking on from the base of the staircase, I hugged My mom, but it felt strange, because now there was a secret between us. Before I could leave, each member of Max's family took a turn hugging me deeply and whispering their love and support in front of my slightly confused mom. In an attempt to explain the oddly intimate behaviour, Max's mom turned to my own and told her how much they appreciated my company, and how delightful it was to have such a polite young man stay with them. My mother beamed with pride at the compliment, though the look she gave me was almost one of disbelief, and through her moment of hubris, she didn't notice the complicit wink that Max's mom gave me.

We got into the car and drove away, in the side mirror, I could see the whole family watching from the doorstep as we turned onto the street and disappeared from their sight. I looked over at my mom, to see if she was still convinced by Miss Longview's fib, but unfortunately, it was clear that she was not.

Soooo… What was all that about? The scepticism in her voice came through loud and clear.

it's… um… well… I didn't know what to say, I wasn't even sure if I was ready, or how to start, it was all so sudden.

My mom could sense that there was something wrong, she pulled off to the side of the road and turned off the car, undid her seatbelt and turned to face me.

Remember Freddy, you promised that you'd talk to me if there was ever anything… She trailed off, leaving an opening for me to come clean, her face stared at me expectantly, but she looked concerned, not mad.

I did promise. And when I thought about how Max's family had taken the news, it gave me renewed hope that it could go just as well with my mom too *"Those who matter don't mind"*, She mattered; she definitely mattered, hopefully she wouldn't mind.

I took a deep breath, but I didn't have Max's confidence, so when it escaped me, it came out more like a whimper. My hands began to shake and my face started to feel really hot. I stared at my lap, because I couldn't look my mom in the eye.

Mom... Another deep breath, my heart felt like it weighed a million pounds... *I'm...* A sigh, I bit my lip to stop myself from crying, this was a big moment, what if she rejected me? What if my mom and I were never the same after this?

What is it sweetheart? You're what? So gentle were her words, like Max's mom earlier that morning.

The faintest squeak of a word escaped my lips, so quiet that a fly passing through would have drowned it out

...gay...

There it was, the moment of truth, I'd said it out loud and now it was judgement time, the hour of reckoning, do or die... But she didn't pause, or falter, she knew how she felt right away, and she made sure to let me know

Hey little-man, look at me... I couldn't lift my head, so she gently directed it towards her own by placing a finger on my chin... *I'm so happy that you told me, and I love you no matter what...* she said that like she'd been practicing... *In fact, I love you even more now, because you can be yourself and I love the real you way more than you can even imagine...* Her own voice had started to crack, as the emotions were getting to her too.

As I looked into her eyes, she left no doubt about the authenticity of that last statement. She gave me that look that only a mother can give that said "don't argue with me, this is final", but where that look usually meant that I was in trouble, this time it warmed my heart.

We hugged for a while, and for the second time that day, I felt like that giant rock had been lifted off of my shoulders.

We didn't talk about it much for the rest of the day, but all afternoon, whenever we locked eyes, my mother seemed to soften her face intentionally, as if she wanted to make sure that I knew this was okay with her, and though it seemed almost exaggerated, it felt nice to see her make an effort.. Later that night the phone rang, and my mom told me that it was Max on the other end as she handed me the receiver. She left the room to give me a bit of privacy.

Hello?

Did you tell her?

He really didn't waste any time.

Yeah, I told her.

So? How did it go? He sounded excited

It went good! She was really cool about it. I'm just glad we don't have to keep this whole thing a secret.

...at home... He finished my sentence, alluding to the circumstances which hadn't changed at school.

Yeah, right, how's this gonna work at school Max?

A sigh came through the phone

I don't know Freddy, I don't want to be a jerk to you at school, but if anyone found out, we'd both be dead...

He hadn't really offered a solution.

...Yeah...

I didn't really have one either.

Maybe we can meet in the woods at lunch! Just hanging out might make it easier to get through the day!

He sounded so hopeful, and for a brief moment I agreed, but then

What about Maggie though? We usually eat lunch every day...

Oh, right... Why don't you invite her? She's cool, we could even tell her!

His usual chipper attitude was in full swing, but he was ignorant to the fact that Maggie had feelings for him. Telling her that Max and I were gay might make her jealous, and she could go around the school telling everyone out of anger. But I couldn't tell him that, not without telling him that she liked him.

I don't know... I'm not sure that's a great idea... Was the best I could come up with.

Yeah, you're right... He responded... *Well, why don't the three of us just have lunch in the woods as friends, she won't think that's weird because of what's been going on with Dylan, and we don't have to tell her about us.*

It was a pretty bulletproof plan, It made a lot of sense, and it didn't expose us to danger, but we still got to spend time together.

Deal! I answered, happy that we'd found a solution.

Great, I can't wait to see you at school!

Me too! Have a good rest of your weekend.

We said goodbye and hung up, the world finally seemed like it might be starting to tilt in my direction for once, everything was working out great, even getting around the bullies at school.

My mom and I finished washing up and she wished me goodnight with a long and almost painful hug before I went off to bed. I fell asleep with images of Max's smile in my head and the memory of his kiss on my lips.

Monday

◆ ◆ ◆

When I arrived at school that Monday, the world felt different, All of the people who had previously just been blurry faces in the crowd seemed to be scrutinizing my every move, like they knew something was up and they were just waiting for me to make a mistake so they could expose my secret. I felt somewhat vulnerable, and seeing Maggie in the schoolyard didn't really help alleviate that.

So? She asked, before she was even close enough for us to be talking.

So, what? Her sentence fragment had left me confused.

As she got closer, she lowered her voice and spoke through her teeth, so any potential lip readers would be thwarted in their attempts to eavesdrop on our conversation.

Does he like me back?

The thought of asking Max if he liked Maggie had completely escaped my mind since we last spoke about it. Max and I had gone through so much that weekend that finding out how he felt about her was the last thing on my mind. And anyways, I knew how he felt about her, he thought of her as a friend, nothing more, I knew that because he was reserving his heart for me, not her. But I couldn't tell her that, not without exposing everything that had gone on at Max's house, so I had to come up with a lie quickly, so as to not arouse suspicion.

Oh shoot, sorry, we were having so much fun that I completely forgot to ask... It wasn't a total lie, we were having fun, and I did forget to ask, but there was definitely a lie of omission there.

Mhm... She responded, placing her hands on her hips and giving me a sideways leer, before rolling her eyes, as if to say "Urgh, boys", but something in her response seemed suspicious, like she wasn't legitimately mad that I hadn't gotten around to ask Max if he liked her.

I was about to prod at her strange behaviour, but the bell rang and we were forced to put this conversation on hold for now, so I shrugged my shoulders as a means of apology and ran off to the building where I quickly made my way to my locker a few doors away from my home-room.

As I was fumbling to get my textbooks out of my locker without toppling the leaning tower of books I kept in there, I saw Max coming down the hall in my direction. He looked up and noticed me, and he gave me a bit of an awkward but covert smile, unsure of what the best course of action would be in this moment, now that we were under the watchful eye of our fellow students.

The look brought a bit of pain to my heart because it served as a stark reminder that our affection for one another still had to remain a secret and because of that, Max would be forced to continue ignoring me in public.

Without a clear resolution, Max turned and walked into our homeroom before anyone could notice our interaction and my heart dropped another level, feeling like I was not only vulnerable to having my secret discovered, but I was alone in dealing with it too, having no one that I could talk to about it at school.

I closed my locker and went into the classroom to take my seat. Dylan was standing between Big-Rig and Scar's desks, the three were talking among themselves, and when they noticed my presence, they stopped talking and shot me a dirty look, to serve as a reminder that I was still in their sights, and that simply being myself was still a punishable offence in their eyes.

I was still feeling pretty low from my awkward interaction with Max, so I didn't notice when Dylan came up behind me and shoved me by the shoulder as he walked by.

Hey fag-boy, how's your girlfriend? Or are you the girlfriend in the relationship? Haha.

He laughed as his own joke and turned around to make sure that Big-Rig and Scar had heard him. They acknowledged him with dumb grins on their faces.

I was in no mood to deal with him in that instant and in a momentary lapse of judgement, I snapped back at him.

Leave me alone Dylan! I almost yelled out, getting the attention of the rest of the class, most of them turning around to see what was going on.

He appeared genuinely surprised at my outburst, but his look quickly turned to anger.

What did you say loser? Dylan got closer to my face as he spoke, it was clear that he didn't appreciate me standing up to him.

In that moment, Miss Friedman walked into the classroom, slightly dishevelled and unaware of the moment she was interrupting, as usual, and instructed everyone to take their seats so the class could start.

The rest of the lesson went on without much drama, but every time I looked over at Dylan, I caught him leering at me, refusing to break his stare. As soon as the bell rang, I got out of the classroom as quickly as I could and went to my next class without stopping to change my books, it didn't seem worth it to stick around and have Dylan confront me in the hallway.

During my next class, I managed to calm down a bit, hoping that Dylan would realize that he had caught me in a bit of a bad mood, and let the whole thing slide for once.

When the lunch bell rang, I ran out to the field to find Maggie so I could catch her up on what had happened, and I saw her sitting in our usual spot, but she wasn't alone, Tristan was standing over her and when he saw me, he turned and walked towards the building without looking back or acknowledging my presence. I tried to figure out what they could possibly have been talking about, but I couldn't come up with any scenario where those two would have had anything to discuss.

What was that about? I asked when I got within earshot of Maggie.

It's... ummm... nothing... She responded, clearly lying.

I raised an eyebrow, hoping to convey that I didn't believe her.

It's stupid... Tristan just.... She trailed off

Tristan just what? I was growing impatient with this game, I really wanted to talk to her about the Dylan situation and see if she agreed that given the circumstances, he might take it easy on me this time.

Well... she took a deep breath...

Something in her demeanour changed, it kind of reminded me of when Max would come up in conversation. Her face turned a bit red and she started to look at her feet, as if she was ashamed of what she was about to say.

...Tristan just... she paused again... *asked me to go to the dance with him on Friday...* She said as she fiddled with there shoelaces

It took me a moment to process her sentence, and by the time I had wrapped my head around it, all of the thoughts in my head had been replaced with the almost inconceivable image of Maggie and Tristan going to the dance together.

With him? I asked in disbelief

I was getting the odd impression that she was considering it, but I thought she didn't like him very much, so it seemed strange to me that she would want to go with him.

Immediately, she got a little defensive

Look, I know we talked about the three of us going together, but Tristan called me this weekend, and we talked for a long time, and he's actually a really nice guy, and I hope you don't hate me for bailing on you and Max.

Bailing? Did she think I would be mad? The fact that she had moved on from Max was the best news I'd heard all day. It explained her strange behaviour from that morning and it made things so much less complicated, not having to keep her feelings for Max a secret was going to alleviate a lot of anxiety for me, but of course she couldn't know that. I thought it wise to play along, I didn't want her to think that this was making me happy, or she might ask more questions for clarification.

I mean... I paused for effect... *I guess it's alright, if you think this is what's going to make you happy...* Again, I paused... *But you're gonna have to be the one to tell Max, he's gonna be pretty bummed that you're bailing on our friend date...*

She clearly hadn't paid attention the whole way through because the look of joy on her face indicated that she was just glad I wasn't pissed. She jumped at my neck, as she was known to do, and proclaimed her satisfaction

Oh thanks Freddy, I knew you'd understand, you're the best!

I wanted to ask her why Tristan had left so suddenly while I was approaching, but I never got the chance to, because at that moment, over Maggie's shoulder, I saw a familiar sight, Dylan and his goons came out of the building, and just like the week before, they spotted us and started heading right in our direction.

My heart stopped as I saw the determination in Dylan's face, all of the morning's fears came flooding back into my head, and Maggie must have felt something shift in me, because she released her grasp on me and turned to face the oncoming danger.

In a moment that felt like a deja-vu, Maggie stood up and pushed her shoulders back while puffing out her chest, standing between me and the bullies, looking prepared to defend me, like a Mama bear protecting her cub.

As they got closer, Maggie yelled out, loud enough for everyone in the schoolyard to hear

Hey back off Dylan, leave him alone.

Dylan more or less ignored her threatening tone and easily pushed her to the side, continuing to make eye contact with me the whole time.

This doesn't concern you... He said, without looking at her.

She was powerless to stand her ground, but she managed to get in an overhand hammer fist to his shoulder, however it didn't seem to phase him, and he continued to approach, looking more and more determined as he got closer.

At this point, Maggie's yelling had gotten a lot of attention and the reality of what was about to happen became clear to everyone in the school-yard, a crowd began to slowly make their way in our direction, not wanting to miss a good confrontation, and everyone seemed hungry for entertainment, particularly because it was going to be at my expense.

I was hoping that he would be rational when he finally got close enough to talk, but the look in his eye wasn't one I'd seen before, it looked like he was ready to fight, not talk.

Get up. He had stopped a foot away from me, his tone left no room for negotiation.

My small frame betrayed me as my shoulders cowered and my muscles refused to show any signs of being there for me in my time of need. I scoured his crowd of goons, but found no trace of Max or Tristan, I guess I was a little relieved that they weren't a part of this at least.

Time slowed as I ran every possible scenario through my head, but none of them seemed to end in me not getting my face smashed in, there were six of them and only one of me, and my odds of getting a fair trial here appeared pretty slim.

GET UP! He repeated himself, this time even more assertively, making the anger in his voice obvious for all to hear.

The spectators that had reached us were looking on with anticipation, I searched their faces for any signs of empathy, perhaps as a group we could defeat Dylan and the idiots, but the blood lust in their eyes indicated that I was all alone in this, they were just here for the show, and my beat down would surely carry a story with it that would haunt me for the rest of my school career.

"Those who mind don't matter..." Scott's words popped into my head in that exact moment, reminding me that Dylan would one day prove himself to be the worthless human that I knew him to be, and that his existence would some day cease mattering to me. I imagined myself being grown up and running a company, maybe one where I was Dylan's boss, and I made him scrub toilets every day because of all the grief he was causing me right now. The thought of making him pay for all of this later brought me the slightest bit of joy and compelled me to accept my fate and get this whole thing over with, once and for all.

As I slowly stood up, my arms and legs trembling in terror, I made a final "all or nothing" attempt at trying to convince Dylan not to beat me up, my words potentially being the only line of defence I had against six much larger and much stronger individuals than myself.

Dylan, im so…

I was going to say that I was sorry that we had gotten off on the wrong foot, and that I was sure that if he gave me a chance, I'd likely prove myself to be a valuable friend in the long run, but I was rudely interrupted by his fist coming into contact with the side of my face.

The hit sent a shock through my body, my brain seemed to shut down completely, as my body hit the ground, and a pretty noticeable wincing "Ouf" came from the crowd of spectators that we had amassed.

As I lay there, trying to regain my ability to see straight, a tingling sensation came from the upper half of my face as a trickle of blood leaked out from the new cut just above my eye and poured down across my forehead before forming a small crimson puddle on the ground in front of me.

The sight of my own blood combined with the

slow onset of pain in my face made my eyes well up, as I felt powerless in that moment, my body not responding to my brain's commands and my tears starting to become evident to everyone around me. A low sob escaped my mouth and I put my hands to my face to hide my crying, but touching my eye proved to be a terrible idea, sending another wave of pain all the way down to my toes.

I heard some high fives and laughter coming from my assailant and his support crew, but as I opened my eyes to give them the best angry look I could muster, I noticed that the crowd of people around were shaking their heads in dis-satisfaction.

It wasn't clear to me in that moment if they were disgusted by Dylan's attack on me or if they were unimpressed by my inability to put up a decent fight, but I was just happy that they didn't seem to be sharing in the celebration that was making it's way through the horde of bullies.

Slowly, some of them started to turn to leave, and through the dissipating crowd, I saw a single fig-ure coming in my direction, but it was impossible to make out his face because the sun was directly behind him, causing a halo effect to form around his head. Without hesitation, his hand reached out to me and I knew instantly that it was Max who was offering me his help to stand up.

I squinted to inspect his face, wanting to make sure that he knew the impact it could have on his reputation to be helping me up, especially since Dylan and his goons were still standing right there, watching the whole thing go down, but his hand didn't falter, so I took it and he hoisted me up to my feet, standing at my side to face the group of boys that was now looking a little dumbfounded.

As we stood there, watching them scratch their heads clearly trying to figure out why anyone would help me out after they had made their opinion of me fairly clear, I noticed that Max had not yet let go of my hand, instead he had changed his grip to interlace his fingers with my own, like every other time that he had wanted me to trust him.

But this felt different, this felt dumb. I had just been punched in the face, and no part of me wanted to repeat that moment, but Max and I holding hands seemed like a sure fire way to have that happen again, sooner rather than later. I looked over at his face to see if I could see any external signs that he'd completely lost his mind, but his look was determined if not defiant, and he appeared like he was just waiting for Dylan to say something, because he had the perfect words to say to him all cued up.

His actions had reignited the interest of the on-lookers from before, and the crowd that had been scattering away had now turned back and started to form again, leaving me to feel less and less comfortable with Max's decision to be holding my hand in this instant.

I tried weakly to pull my hand away, but he tightened his grip and looked over at me with his determined face and his calming blue eyes as if to say "don't worry, I've got this", so I opted to blindly trust his plan and I let our hands fall back between us, before he turned back towards Dylan and continued his stare down.

What the hell is going on? Dylan spoke first, still unable to comprehend what was happening.

If you have a problem with Freddy, you have a problem with me. Max spat back, without a hint of fear or hesitation in his voice.

He was going to get us both killed.

Ah man, don't do this... Dylan pleaded... *You're cool, and he's...* he paused, looking around to make sure everyone was paying attention... *well, he's a fag...* He said that so plainly, like it was a well known fact.

He's not a fag... Max shot back... *He's gay, and who cares?*

Wait, what? Did Max just out me? What the actual f...

...And plus... He continued, interrupting my thought... *So am I*

The whole world felt like it had stopped spinning. Everyone grew quiet for what seemed like an eternity, Dylan's face looked like it was trying to process what Max was saying, how could a cool guy like him be gay? It didn't make any sense, and that was obvious in his expression. Then, in an instant, a look of relief came across his face and he smiled from ear to ear as he let out a deep guttural laugh.

Hahaha, you got me, trying to make me think you're gay, that's a good one dude... Now get out of the way so I can finish kicking his ass.

Max looked frustrated that Dylan thought he was joking, so without warning, he turned to me, grabbed my head with both of his hands and planted a kiss directly on my lips. It felt like the perfect mixture of a death wish and a knife in the back, but I couldn't help but succumb to the kiss, Max's lips were so soft, and his kiss didn't seem like it had as much defiance behind it as his words had indicated, instead it was sweet and comforting, like he was trying to make this whole thing seem normal to everyone, not like he was just trying to prove a point.

It only lasted for a moment, but for that moment, the whole world disappeared, the crowd that had formed around us felt like they were off in the distance, miles away, and Dylan and his goons didn't even exist in the world that Max had created for us by connecting our lips together. For the briefest nano-second, I felt safe, Max and I were one with each other, and the super-being that we formed was stronger than everybody else in the world combined.

As I snapped back to reality, I heard a loud gasp echo throughout our audience, and I was left feeling drained of any thoughts of wrongdoing or shame. I was proud that Max had kissed me in front of everyone, I wanted them all to know how I felt about him and it felt good to have him trying to express it too. It didn't even seem important that there might be social ramifications for what we had just done.

As the reality of the situation settled in, Dylan looked over his shoulder to ensure that he still had everyone's support, while he prepared to attack us both, but to his dismay, the people standing around us had taken our side and turned on him, and were now starting to heckle him for having hit a gay kid.

How dare you?

What did he ever do to you?

What's wrong with you?

Dylan turned to plead his case, but was met with angry stares and crossed arms. The number of protesters to his cause was a little overwhelming compared to him and his five idiot friends. He looked like he was about to say something, but relented, seeing that his case would not sway anyone, so he huffed loudly and walked off angrily, taking his goons with him as he left.

This isn't over... he yelled back over his shoulder, as he walked away

Yes it is... Responded someone anonymous from the huddle around us, causing a few laughs and deflating Dylan's threat.

The crowd turned back towards Max and I, still holding hands, and each one did their best to give us a look of acknowledgement or a pat on the back in support as they slowly started to turn and walk away, satisfied that the danger had passed, leaving the two of us to process what had just gone down. Without having said a word to either of us, they had easily conveyed that they were cool with what we were, and that they were ready to side with us if Dylan ever gave us any more problems.

Well that wasn't nearly as bad as I thought it would be... Max said, bringing me back into the present moment, trying to break the tension.

I noticed that in the middle of everything, my fear had made me begin to squeeze his hand tighter and tighter and that now both of our knuckles had turned white from the added pressure. I eased off slightly, apologizing by bowing my head, and scoffed softly at his words.

Yeah, I guess it could have been way worse... I tried to sound fully relieved, but the terror in my heart hadn't quite finished subsiding yet.

Max turned towards me with a smile to acknowledge my attempt, but it quickly faded as he saw my now swelling eye, and the trail of drying blood running down my cheek.

Hey, we gotta get you to the nurse. He said, very seriously, leaving no room for negotiation.

I nodded my head, letting him lead the way to the

nurses office, where she cleaned me up and gave me some ice for my cut, before proclaiming that it wasn't that bad and that it would heal nicely on it's own in a few days.

Principal Newridge's office

◆ ◆ ◆

The next day I was called into the principal's office and when I got there, I saw Dylan and his parents as well as my mom, who were all sitting quietly waiting for me to arrive. Principal Newridge asked me to sit down and then proceeded to tell me that Dylan had something to say to me. We all looked over at Dylan expectantly and he rolled his eyes and sighed before pulling a crumpled piece of paper out of his pocket and slowly unfolding it, the loud crunch of the paper only adding to the awkwardness in the otherwise silent room. Dylan cleared his throat and sat up straight before speaking, giving the impression that he was being genuine.

Freddy, I'm sorry that I punched you in the face yesterday, and I promise that it won't happen again.

He looked over at his father, who was clearly seething in his chair, his tight shirt showed off his buff physique and it was clear that he was a military man. His cold demeanour made it clear that he was not impressed with his son's lacklustre attempt at an apology. Seeing Dylan and his father interact made me realize that Dylan's actions towards me were most likely him just mimicking his fathers actions towards him. I felt for him in that moment, because I finally saw him as a human, and it may not have justified Dylan's actions, but it certainly gave them context.

Somebody in the room spoke to pull me out of my thoughts.

Is that it? Principal Newridge asked, almost sounding surprised that Dylan had needed to write that down to remember it.

Dylan looked at him almost defiantly, and raised his shoulders as if to say "what more do you want?"

Ahem... alright then... Frederick, is there anything that you would like to tell Dylan at this time?

I hadn't expected any of this, let alone the opportunity to tell him how I felt in front of his parents, but I had no anger left towards him, I felt sorry that he was this way. Something really awful was clearly going on in his life that made him this way, and it made me understand why he would need an outlet, even if that outlet was my face. In a lot of ways, I felt safe now, the whole school knew our secret and had accepted us, and even sort of offered to help us out if Dylan and his goons gave us any more grief, so I had no reason to fear him anymore, and taking away the fear made him seem powerless, so I felt like he'd lost already.

Not really... I said before turning to address Dylan directly... *I appreciate that you're sorry Dylan, and I'm sorry too, I'm sorry we got off on the wrong foot, and I'm sorry that things got this bad between us, I'm really a nice guy and I bet that you are too, it's just a shame that we couldn't just be friends.*

Everyone in the room seemed taken back by what I had said, I think that the swollen state of my face had made them anticipate much sharper words from me, but I just didn't see a point in escalating this any further, I wanted this whole thing to be over and for everyone to just go on with their lives.

Okay, ummm, thank you Frederick... Principal Newridge said, sounding shocked, before turning to Dylan's parents... *Now unfortunately, due to Frederick's sexual orientation, what Dylan did yesterday is classified as a hate crime, which means that my hand is forced by the school's charter and I must immediately expel Dylan from our premises and ask that he never return...*

Dylan's mom gasped in shock and his father had a vein that was throbbing pretty hard in his forehead, indicating that he was furious with his son, and Dylan just sat there with his arms crossed, trying to look like he didn't care, but it was obvious that he was hurting inside. Then once the room had settled down a bit, Principal Newridge turned to my mom and continued to deliver the news

As for you Misses Miller, Dylan's actions towards your son were unacceptable, and from the school's perspective, the punishment is clear, however, I am obliged to inform you that since it qualifies as a hate crime, you would be well within your legal right to press charges against his family and the school, if you chose to do so.

Again, Dylan's mom gasped, thought this time, she held her hand to her mouth and began to cry, seeing that this whole situation had only just begun for them, both from the school's standpoint, but now also from a legal perspective. Dylan's father just did his best to swallow his anger, but his fists were clenched so tight that his knuckles began to turn white and the vein in his forehead looked like it was about to explode, he kept looking over at Dylan, who was now cowering in his chair, and it seemed like he was restraining himself from giving him a good punishment of his own, right then and there.

My mom looked over at me with her eyebrows raised, it was evident that she hadn't even considered the possibility of legal action, and she was trying to gauge my reaction to see if I thought we should move forward with this.

I don't know... what do you think honey? She asked me somewhat awkwardly, I could tell that she didn't really want to put me on the spot, but it was clear that Dylan and his family were holding their breaths, waiting for me to deliver my verdict on whether or not Dylan was about to become a criminal, so this seemed like the best time to address the issue.

This whole thing seemed unfair to Dylan, two days earlier, I would have gladly sent him to jail, but the circumstances had changed, he was no longer a threat to me, so I just saw him as someone who was enduring the consequences of a stupid mistake, and as much as I hated to admit it, he looked like he was pretty terrified of his dad at this point, so turning this into a bigger issue was basically sending him to the guillotine.

The room was very quiet as I deliberated.

I don't think that's necessary mom, he said he was sorry and he promised to leave me alone, and I believe him. And anyways... I said, turning to principal Newridge... *he didn't know I was gay when he punched me, so it wasn't really a "hate crime" if you ask me, it was just two guys working stuff out... I don't think he should really even be expelled.*

For the second time, an air of surprise was plastered on everyone's faces as a collective feeling of hopeful anticipation was felt in the room, followed closely by Principal Newridge seeing the opportunity to exploit a loophole so that he wouldn't have to expel a student and face a lawsuit.

Is that right Dylan? Did you know about Frederick's sexual orientation when you hit him? He was almost holding his breath as he posed the question.

Dylan seemed most surprised out of anyone in the room, we both knew what he had said to me and that this was kind of a lie, and it was obvious that he was having a hard time believing that after everything he'd done to me, I was coming up to bat for him on this.

Uhh... no, I had no idea... he said as he looked over at me, his face looked like he was unsure if he should trust me in this moment, or if this was all part of a bigger master plan.

Principal Newridge scratched his head a bit and

sat back in his chair, Dylan's parents looked like there might almost be a bit of hope for leniency here so they started holding their breath again.

Well then... In light of this new information, I guess this is no longer a case of hate crimes, and just a simple case of schoolyard violence, which carries a mandatory punishment of two week's suspension and the cancellation of all extra-curricular activities for Dylan for one whole month... He turned to Dylan... *So that means no dance, no sports and no field trips, is that understood?*

Dylan nodded his head, with him and his parents again releasing a collective sigh of relief, Dylan was smiling like he'd just been pardoned from death row.

Very well... Continued Principal Newridge... *I'll have the expulsion forms shredded and the suspension forms drawn up by Miss Wilkins right away...* He turned to me... *Thank you Frederick for your honesty, you may go back to class now...* Then he looked over at my mother... *Thank you for coming in Miss Miller, we will keep a close eye on this situation and be sure to notify you if anything other issues arise...* He reassured her, and then looked at Dylan's family... *And you folks may wait in the lounge while Miss Wilkins prepares the forms for you to sign.*

He finished his speech with an air of finality, like only a principal can, making it clear that we were all done here.

As my mom and I were walking out of the office, Dylan caught up to me and put a hand on my shoulder so I would stop and turn around, all of the adults around stood quietly and watched to see what would happen next, but I didn't feel threatened in that moment, so I decided to indulge him.

Hey... um... thanks for that... That seemed hard for him to say... *I thought you were a rat, but...* He paused, like he was struggling to push these words out... *I guess I was wrong about you.*

My mouth fell open, I was floored by his sincerity, it really felt like we had turned a corner, and all of a sudden the air in the room felt much lighter. I smiled at him genuinely...

It's all good man, everyone's wrong sometimes, that's how we learn... I heard my dad's words coming out of my mouth without my consent, but they had been better than anything I could have come up with in that moment, so I embraced them like they were my own.

Dylan took a moment to absorb the words and

smiled back before patting my shoulder lightly, as if to say "you're alright kid", before turning back to go sit with his parents, who were now beaming with pride at their son's latest actions. It had been an emotional meeting for them, and I think they were just happy that he had a two week suspension instead of an expulsion and a criminal record, so the tension in their faces had definitely decreased since they had been in the office.

As I was about to leave for my class, my mom asked me to walk her to her car, which I thought was weird but I obliged her anyways, and when we got there, she stopped before opening the door and turned towards me, which is when I saw her misty eyes for the first time, I couldn't quite figure out why she was on the verge of crying, so I asked her what was wrong.

I'm just... she paused slightly to get a grip... *I'm just so proud of you Freddy, that was so mature and decent back there...* A tear rolled out of the corner of her eye and down her cheek... *I really couldn't ask for a better son...* She put a hand behind my head and pulled me in for a hard hug... *I only wish your dad could have seen that...* She paused briefly... *He'd be so proud of you little man.*

That last sentiment had really hit me deep, the thought of making my dad proud was pretty heavy for me in that moment and I couldn't help but follow in my mom's footsteps and start to cry into her shoulder.

Friday

◆ ◆ ◆

When Friday finally came, Maggie showed up at my house after school so we could get ready for the dance together. She had picked a few things for me out of my closet, and was standing behind me, helping me do up my bowtie in front of the mirror when the doorbell rang. Realizing that our ride was here, Maggie turned me around and we shared a look of excitement before heading down the hall towards the front door.

My mom was already there, holding open the door and Max and Tristan were standing in the entrance, both looking anxious but handsome. When Max and I locked eyes, his smile lit up and he looked as happy to see me dressed up as I was to see him.

My mom wouldn't let us leave without getting a few pictures of the four of us in our formal wear, and when that was all done and she wished us a good night, we walked out into the fresh fall air and made our way to the car where

Max's mom was waiting with the engine running.

As we walked behind Tristan and Maggie, Max slowed down so they would be out of earshot when he leaned over and said in a slightly quiet voice

You look really nice Freddy, I like your bowtie

I was smitten by his compliment, and my face turned a bit red

Thanks, Maggie picked it out... You look really nice too Max... I said, staring at my feet

He smiled at me, but didn't have time to say anything else before we got to the car, where Tristan was holding the door open to let Maggie have the front seat and the three of us piled into the back together, with Max sitting in the middle between Tristan and I.

During the car ride, Tristan spent most of the time talking, and the rest of us just sat quietly and let him fill the silence, and when we got to the school, everyone got out of the car and thanked Max's mom for the ride.

Tristan and Maggie ran off almost immediately, wanting to catch up with some friends they saw going in, but not before Maggie asked me to save her a dance later, to which I gladly agreed.

As the car was pulling away, leaving Max and I standing together in front of the school, about to enter the dance as a couple, Max looked over at me with a slight look of worry in his eye.

Are you ready for this? He asked, almost sounding like he expected me to say no.

I took a deep breath for courage

There's no time like the present... I guess

Max smiled his reassuring smile and took my hand in his, he looked into my eyes but didn't say a word, then, without warning, he leaned in and quickly placed a kiss on my lips, causing us both to smile, knowing that we could do that in public now. He turned and pulled me towards the front doors of the school, where we handed our tickets to Hellen Birch, the student body president, and made our way into the gymnasium.

The rafters were covered in streamers and balloons, and the walls were lined with harvest-themed posters. There was a table near the dj with a punchbowl and some cups on it, being closely monitored by Miss Wilkins, and the music was playing loudly, with the main lights mostly lowered and the racks of party lights shining colourful laser beams all over the walls and floor.

The room was already pretty full when we entered, and as we walked in, it seemed like just about everybody stopped and turned to see us at the entrance holding hands with one another.

A moment of doubt crossed my mind as I thought this might not have been a good idea... Maybe everyone was just being nice to us the other day because they all hated Dylan so much, but what if they weren't actually accepting of us.

Just as I was beginning to panic on the inside, one by one, the other students went back to their own dancing and before I knew it, no one was paying any attention to us anymore. In the crowd, I saw Maggie and Tristan dancing and she was waving us over to join them.

We all danced together for a while while I thought about how funny it was that two weeks ago, I had been so nervous about being accepted at this school and that now, I was out of the closet and I had a bunch of new friends and I'd never felt so much joy all at once.

As the upbeat music came to an end, we heard the first few notes of a slow song coming on and the spastic twirl of the party lights mellowed out. A lot of people left the dance floor, being too shy to ask their crushes for a dance, and I got nervous as Max turned towards me with a look on his face that was insinuating that he wanted a dance.

It seemed like a make or break moment for our reputation, up until this point, the concept of Max and I being gay was mostly hypothetical to our classmates, but this would be a moment where they would see us intimate and vulnerable, and I wasn't sure how much I wanted to put myself through that.

As if Max could read my mind, and could see that I was in need of some reassurance, he gently took my hand and pulled me in, wrapping his arms around me, giving me a feeling of protection and he looked me in the eye with his patented smile before whispering

It's okay Freddy, they don't mind

He was alluding to his fathers words and it made me relax a little, allowing myself to enjoy the feeling of Max holding me as the singer in the song talked about love and we shuffled our feet around slowly.

All around, I could see people staring at us, but they weren't snickering like I had expected, they had smiles of acceptance on their faces, and a few of the girls were looking on enviously, persuading their dates to ask them onto the dance floor. Before long, most of the students had coupled up and were now surrounding us, allowing us to get lost in the crowd, making us feel like we were all the same, and as Max put a hand on the back of my head, pulling me into his shoulder, I revelled in his warm embrace, letting myself get lost in the words of the song and the feeling of pure joy in my heart.

It had been an emotional couple of weeks, a lot of things had happened, but it felt kind of relieving to think that it might be coming to an end, or a new beginning, one where everything was relatively normal, and no bullies were trying to kill me at school, and no secrets were eating away at me on the inside, and one where Max and I were free to explore our feelings for each other, without the fear of being prosecuted by our peers.

All of a sudden, it felt like the clouds had parted and my heart felt warm and bright like the sun was shining directly on it.

THE END

Made in the USA
Monee, IL
15 February 2021